The Ship of Fools

The Ship of Fools

a novel by

Cristina Peri Rossi

translated from the Spanish

by Psiche Hughes

readers international

The title of this book in Spanish is *La nave de los locos*, first published
in 1984 in Spain by Editorial Seix Barral, S.A., Barcelona.

English translation first published by Readers International, Inc. in
the United States and Allison & Busby in Great Britain.

Cover art by Uruguayan artist Joaquin Torres Garcia (1874–1949)
Design by Jan Brychta
Typesetting by Grassroots Typeset, London N3
Printed and bound in Great Britain by
Richard Clay Ltd, Bungay, Suffolk

Library of Congress Catalog Card Number: 88-61390

ISBN 0-930523-53-9 Hardcover
ISBN 0-930523-54-7 Paperback

Life is a voyage of experiment made against our will.
Fernando Pessoa

The marriage of reason and nightmare that has dominated the twentieth century has given birth to an ever more ambiguous world.
J.G. Ballard

Nothing destroys us more surely than the silence of another human being.
George Steiner

Ecks: The Journey, I

In the dream I heard an order: "You will come to the city—describe it." So I asked, "How shall I know what is meaningful from what is not?"

Later I found myself in a field, winnowing wheat from chaff. Under a grey sky and lilac clouds, the work was hard, but simple. Time didn't exist, rather it had turned to stone. I kept working in silence until she appeared. Stooping over the field, she took pity on a weed and I, to please her, added it to the harvest. Then she did the same for a stone. After, she begged mercy for a mouse. When she had gone, I was confused. The straw seemed more beautiful and the grain, unyielding. Doubt overwhelmed me.

I stopped my work. Since then wheat and chaff have mixed. Under the grey sky the horizon is a smudge, and no voice answers.

Ecks: The Journey, II

Also thou shalt not oppress a stranger: for ye know the heart of a stranger, seeing ye were strangers in the land of Egypt(Exodus 23:9)

A stranger. Ecks. Estranged. Expelled from the womb of earth. Eviscerated: once more to give birth. *Thou shalt not oppress a stranger*. Yes. You. You. You. You who are not. You know. You all know. We are beginning to know. How it beats. How. The heart of the stranger. The outsider. Looking in. The intruder. The fugitive. The vagabond. The lost one. Who would know him? Who would know, perchance, how fares the soul of the stranger? Sad? Resentful? Has he a soul at all? *Seeing ye were strangers in the land of Egypt*.

The ship's siren had begun to howl exactly at line eighteen of *The Illiad*, Canto VI: "*Great-hearted son of Tidis, why ask you of my lineage?*" Thus Glaucus confronting Diomedes. Sirens: legendary maidens living on an isle between Circe's domain and the reef of Scilla, who with their enchanting voices lured the sailors. He remarked this because it was the fifth day of the journey and the second port of call. The Beautiful Passenger approached him. For want of anything better to say, her voice purring like that of a white cat bored with the sea, she inquired,

"What are you reading?"

He informed her, noting carefully that there were many different versions. In others, for example, Glaucus says, "*Why do you question me about my past?*" And the sirens, they weren't the same either. Salvatore Quasimodo had begun a new translation of *The Illiad*; he hadn't finished the task, but there were four beautiful cantos. Where? Ah yes, in the hold of the ship, boxed up, many hundreds of miles to sea in some direction, east or west, north or south. He had never been well versed in geography—or in oceans.

"*Is this really your first voyage?*" the Beautiful Passenger had asked on that fifth day. Green eyes and wide sea, swinging hips and plunging necklines. The sea was rolling like the water in a glass. Or the ship was. The ship was a glass floating on the high tide.

"Really, it's my first," he answered. Now he would have to give all sorts of explanations. "Of course," he said, trying to extricate himself—from the past, from the future, from further questions, from uncertainty, "I've read about all manner of voyages possible in books."

She kept silent, but looked at him with curiosity, a curiosity so intense and challenging that he became restless.

"I might even say," he added with a smugness that only timidity could excuse, "I've already read about this journey five times over."

He had read of this journey. The narrow ship's corridors painted an ochre yellow like those of a hospital; the sea smell; the doors of the passenger cabins numbered like cubicles for the sick; the tourist-class bar, with its red leather stools and spotlights glowing orange, the stage on which the small orchestra regularly played the same tunes, slightly off-key. Dated, nostalgic music of doubtful origin, suitable for all ages, all passengers, for any mood: *Star Dust, Something to Remember, Let's Swing*

Down to Havana, Tango Time. Perhaps one night they would introduce something new, execute (literally) *Diamonds for You*.

He had read of this journey. The Beautiful Passenger, languidly parading in her green dress, her affected curiosity which would lead, inevitably, to a shaded cabin; dancing the *bolero* with grace and just a touch of pro-vocation, that slow *bolero* of Los Panchos, the long steps made longer like the "o" of *amoor*, or hips moving (a precise swing like the roll of the sea) in a *rumba* which seemed to have a depressing effect on no one but him. He felt he was travelling not in space but backwards in time.

He had read of this journey. At breakfast time the corridors leading to the dining hall are crowded with peo-ple leaning on the railings, showing signs of a bad night, because the sea has been rough ("My dear, I could see the waves rising in the mirror. Everything fell out of my bag and I couldn't find my seasick pills"). At meals, the passengers can hardly hide their greed. Anxious to get the fullest return on the price paid for their tickets, they look in vain at the menu where the same dishes reappear, hoping to spot an unexpected dessert or the champagne that never comes.

He had read of this journey. The dances lasting until dawn; the officers directing professional glances at legs and calves, and upward to thighs and hips, while slowly lighting American cigarettes and repeating that the ship is a replica of that other world which they are missing during the fortnight's voyage. Smaller and meaner this world, like all reproductions to scale, yet ruled by the same laws, with its hunters and hunted, with its ranks, social classes and commerce. Now the orchestra attacks

The Third Man. Half-heartedly the lights travel around the dance floor to seek out the saxophonist playing solo—sex and rum, pudgy hands covered with a slight blue fuzz. Couples move sluggishly, oppressed by alcohol and the sea swell, by the drifting, the endless water, by brief and fugitive encounters. There's something of the ghetto here, of prison, and the Beautiful Passenger is swaying alone in the centre of the dance floor. For the moment she does not want a partner. Ecks orders another whiskey, and looks at her as she glides and turns beneath the paper garlands and Chinese lanterns which remind him of his childhood. After the lights go out, they'll hang like forgotten trophies, lonely witnesses, spent fireflies*.

The night does not ride freely on board. There are rules, codes, rites to be performed. After twelve, indifferent waiters (they despise the tourist-class passengers because they never leave tips and are always hungry) place trays of pizza on the long white table in the ballroom. The excited dancers throw themselves upon the food like starving refugees. *The stranger shall thou not oppress: for ye are strangers*. The dance floor is empty, the garlands droop; everybody is congregating around the pizza and the red sauce gashes on the

---

* *Entomological note*: "The lover's nest in your hair," liberally rendered by Vercingetorix from the popular *tango* as, "the spider's nest in your hair". To Ecks's friend it seemed odd that the great Carlos Gardel would hymn the insect life scurrying about under a lady's coiffure, but in matters of the heart Vercingetorix was surprisingly catholic, and having tried out his variation several times in a deep, discordant baritone, he flatly refused to modify it. So at night in the cafés on the square he would fix his gaze on the hair of female passersby, trying to discover beneath the tints and curls the dark fascination of the spider's nest.

tablecloth. Only the Beautiful Passenger does not turn toward the trays. She is looking at him, inquisitively, from afar, and he receives her look like a signal, a light on the high seas, the green beacon in the darkness to guide sailors. He is aware that there is another journey within this journey.

A sailor pins on the notice board the program of tomorrow's activities: *Saturday: 7 o' clock, early Mass*. Who goes to Mass on board? Probably the old couple in cabin A 26, a toothless old lady and her sick husband. Ecks has twice shared a table with them. The old man complains about his stomach, that almost everything he eats disagrees with him. The old lady smiles understandingly, looks around and explains to the rest of the passengers (indifferent, bent over their plates), "He's seasick you know. The movement of the sea affects him."

Is she taking him to die in his own land? To die in the village where he was born? His face is yellow, he has greenish rings under his eyes and talks little. The old woman chews slowly, nibbling at her food. Without hurrying, without greed, she always finishes her meal, though she is the last to get up from the table, the waiter eying her impatiently.

Like a grey bird she devours all that is put before her. The old man can't eat; he looks at his food and his face acquires a waxy complexion like that of a mannequin. "Eat, dear, eat," insists his wife. And the spaghetti sauce seems more red, more aggressive, more unhealthy than before. Tiring of the spectacle—while the others were swabbing the bottoms of their plates with lumps of bread—Ecks told her, "Take him to the doctor on board and get him a special menu."

The woman looked at him in surprise. Then she

6

looked at her husband as if for the first time she seriously considered the possibility of his being ill, becoming less acceptable, offensive almost, a possibility which would have nothing to do with the old man and yet would alter the order of their lives. She then turned her eyes to the plate swimming with red sauce, steaming and over-spiced, seemed to lament the waste, and answered, "No. It's the sea. The sea. He's seasick."

He thought how unfortunate it would be to have a funeral on board.

From 10 to 12: assorted activities. In the tourist saloon the elderly passengers doze on the brown leather armchairs, their backs to the sea. Heads bowed, legs sprawling like broken dolls. At low tables others play at cards or dominoes. The reading room is deserted. On the first day Ecks had browsed the shelves with curiosity; the shelves of dark varnished wood, cased in glass lest a brusque dip throw their contents to the floor. There was nobody in the room, nor would he find anyone there on subsequent days. A piece of paper glued to the wall gave instructions in the event—remote enough—of a passenger wishing to borrow a book: "*Address yourself to one of the ship's officers, give the number of your passport and the title of the book you wish to read. The book will then be checked out and issued to you upon receipt.*"

The Lives of the Saints, The Adventures of Robin Hood, A Gardening Manual, Ramona, The Pyramids of Egypt, Adventures at Sea, The Betrothed, Hamlet, Prince of Denmark. The room was intimate and quiet; he remained there a while. There was a long oval table of dark wood, three lamps with green shades projected a clear and pleasant light on the elyptical shapes in its surface. The walls were covered with prints of ships—a sixteenth-century frigate with yellow spars and open sails, a French brig, a double-decked warship with sixty cannon, a fifteenth-century caravel bearing a great red cross on its flag. Though lonely, it seemed to him quite a suitable room for reading, closed to the threatening sound of the sea. A room for smoking a pipe, for writing about long voyages which forever begin and never come to an end. There was also a plan of the cabins showing the different levels of the boat in which they were travelling.

He had read of this journey. He had never wanted to travel.

On the slippery deck the sun comes and goes, and there are always crew members painting some part of the structure, carefully matching the colour. They stand on wooden towers like those devices used in the Middle Ages to attack fortresses. Ecks had the impression that the ship was a pile of wood on a pedestal, slowly and heavily advancing through the waters which fanned open in front of it.

He had read of this journey. The orchestra was playing the last notes of *My Foolish Heart* and he had just thrown his cigarette to the floor when the Beautiful Passenger came towards him, fixing him coolly with her large green eyes.

"Chess?" she said.

Meekly he followed her to the game room, which at this time of night was empty. Walking behind her, he let the feline sway of her hips draw him on like perfume.

They sat at a comfortable table covered in felt. Through the side window the thick black sea was invisible. She distributed the pieces with assurance. Right away he knew, "I've lost." The game had not yet been set up, but already he seemed to have no chance. With a keen sense of impending failure, he set out his line of luckless pawns who would soon desert him. Hers were fine bishops and bronzed knights who moved with strength and purpose over the board. "I shall lose," he thought. "I've already lost."

An officer in white uniform came in and stopped to watch the match. The officer was looking at the woman, who was looking at the board—her long, slim hands operating with precision. In a single movement, as a surgeon slits and opens the skin, she moved deeply into his territory, took out his bishop, eliminating any dangers to herself, and plunged ahead, always advancing. "You'll lose. Whatever move you make, you've already lost," the officer's knowing look seemed to imply.

Disconcerted, Ecks could only effect a weak defensive manoeuvre with his queen. Then he waited. He saw how the eyes of the officer were appraising the Beautiful Passenger, taking in her thick, well-groomed hair, the wide shoulders, that tanned back, those firm legs—how her delicate fingers marshalled the encroaching forces.

He retreated to relieve his king, but check became mate.

As she was leaving, the officer invited her for a drink, but she refused and instead took Ecks by the arm.

"So this is your first voyage," she said, as if resuming their previous conversation, and this time he was ready to follow her to her cabin.

When she closed the door and began to remove her dress without taking off her shoes, Ecks thought that he had read about this also.

He had read of this journey: standing at the side of the ship after ten days of continuous sailing. To the west the sea lay enfolded in white lace, like a baby in a shawl; to the east the water was viscous and covered with vein-like strings of vegetation, an amniotic bag swelling under the weak sunlight. To the south spread the wakes of the boat, paths of water no one would tread, lost avenues in a lost sea. To the north, upon the dark oily surface swirled traces of a prehistoric beast trapped in a peaty marsh; an exhausted, last dinosaur no longer able to raise its head.

The child was there too, a little boy no more than three years old. His father, a tall, ungainly man with a large bony head, was trying to convince him that they would soon come to the city. There was some wind and the white shirt of the man waved on the high sea, a flag without an answer. A few salty drops were wetting the rails, the red-striped deck chairs ballooned empty like abandoned tents. The child was grasping the dark trousers of his father (mast against the wind), and playing the tyrant:

"I want to get off! I want to go out in the streets!"

Ecks looked at the vast avenue of water, its surface endlessly traversed over time (the child still crying. "Want to go out! In the streets!'') He touched the cold metal of the railing, whose fresh paint the sea salt was already scarring, and peered beneath the waves looking for the crusted relics of submerged cities. Like an ancient priest bending over still-warm viscera, he pointed out to the child:

"Down there is a city full of streets with trees shaped like fishes, and the octopuses turn like carousels. There are water-flowers and houses with glassy walls, green swords and lights that shine all night to keep any monsters away. But you have to know how to look, for it is well-hidden.''

Soberly the boy dug in his pockets and took out a piece of pale blue glass which a sailor had given him one morning to stop him crying. Showing it to Ecks, he said,

"I think I will be able to see it with this.''

ON-BOARD BULLETIN

Monday, 12th of June

Last night at 8:30 the long-awaited party took place in honour of sighting the Straits of Gibraltar. It was a well-attended and delightful occasion. The flower of poetry sprang to the lips of our famous passenger Don Joaquin Arias, who recited with deep feeling verses from his own pen. (*A Shaeffer, in silver, latest clip-on model which also gives the day and month and plays a soft melody to awaken the wife of Sr Arias, a lady inclined to over-eating and sleeping.*) His reward was an elegant certificate signed by the Captain, officers, waiters, cook, musicians and passengers. (*Ecks did not sign because he objected to the rhyme of the last line. He excused himself on grounds of principle.*) Don Joaquin was attended by his wife and daughter, both attired in their most elegant finery.

On the same evening, the sixty-fifth birthday of Don Benito Alonso, another of our eminent passengers, was commemorated in the presence of his closest relatives. Don Benito Alonso is travelling back to his native country. He addressed a few moving words, recalling his years spent in America and the great sacrifices which had accompanied his brilliant business career, rising from a mere waiter to proprietor of a chain of restaurants. He described how, fulfilling a long cherished dream, he looked forward to a triumphant return to the place of his birth. The passengers had made the charming gesture of getting up a collection to buy him a handsome silk tie.

Tomorrow, a costume parade will take place and the prize, consisting of a silver cutlery box, will be awarded to the person displaying the most original disguise. The choice will be decided by the volume of public applause. A ball will follow to the strains of our wonderful orchestra. To enhance the festivities, A and B decks will be decorated with garlands.

Present situation:

At noon yesterday our position was 20 degrees latitude North and 94 degrees 15 longitude West. The weather is cloudy with light to moderate East wind and a slightly disturbed sea. Temperature: 12° centigrade.

BY MIDNIGHT THE LIGHTS OF GIBRALTAR WILL BE IN SIGHT.

The Tapestry of the Creation, I

The work is hung in such a way that the visitor, observing it either from the long seat of carved wood placed in front, or standing a few feet away, can see it fully extended, one's gaze travelling from left to right or from the top downwards. * As happens with certain paintings, the onlooker is drawn into the composition. With enough perseverance, he comes to dwell within it. Everything is so arranged that man can feel in harmony with the design, become part of its embroidered universe, at one with the creatures fantastic and real: birds with fish tails, winged dogs, lions with tortoise shells and serpents with wolves' muzzles; angels catching fish and winds issuing from fat wineskins. The observer— mirroring the man portrayed in threads of many colours—is invited to take his part in the creation,

* This *Tapestry of the Creation* hangs in the Cathedral of Gerona. Ecks saw it on one of his journeys and was much affected. Unlike later medieval tapestries rich with pagan and courtly elements as well as Christian symbolism, this is more austere, the product of a religious system, a world, that is perfectly concentric and ordered. But such harmony assumes the destruction of those aspects of reality which oppose it; thus it is almost always purely symbolic. Ecks studied the tapestry as one might read an old legend whose rhythm fascinates, but which evokes no nostalgia.

alongside the ox with its parrot-head and the sword sprouting leaves. And so too, without leaving the confines of the weaving, he feels himself to be at the very centre of creation, while still in touch with its borders and frontiers. Art like this beckons man to live within its world, freed from the sins of the other one.

When it was first woven in the eleventh or twelfth century, the tapestry must have measured six metres in length, but only three metres sixty-five survive. The passage of time—whole epochs in revolt—has destroyed almost half of it. But the overall structure of the work, the strands of coloured thread and the remaining, mutilated fragments allow us to recontruct the composition and imagine the themes depicted in the missing parts. What one admires in the work, besides the fine execution, handsome texture and harmony of colours, is this structure—a structure so symmetical, so dependable that even when incomplete, it is possible to recreate the whole, if not on the cathedral wall, then within the framework of our imagination.

There the missing parts unfurl, fragments intimating the larger harmony of the universe. What we love in any structure is a vision of the world that gives order to chaos, an hypothesis which is comprehensible and restores our faith, atoning for our having fled and scattered before life's brutal disorder. We value in art the exercise of mind and emotion that can make sense of the universe without reducing its complexity. Immersed in such art one could live one's life, engaged in a perfectly rational discourse whose meaning cannot be questioned because it resides in an image containing the whole universe.

What surprises and will always surprise is the

notion that a single mind could conceive of such a convincing and pleasing structure, moreover a happy one, a structure which as well as being a metaphor is also a reality.

Ecks, III: Man is Woman's Past

Bearing in mind the figures for life expectancy established by the World Health Organization (WHO), which he had read in a travel magazine during the flight from Madrid to Toronto, and always assuming that he falls within the average, Ecks supposes he will go on living until he is seventy.[1] This discounts the possibility of speeding cars (as a pedestrian he is only indifferently attentive), the sudden emergence of fanatical generals, the threat from smoking. "Bring my death a bit closer, will you?" With that phrase Vercingetorix used to scrounge for cigarettes, adopting a trait Ecks noticed was common among his compatriots of the River Plate—turning anxiety into a black joke.

In the years that might go by until that fatal day, Ecks would prefer to remain seated in the stalls at the Rex Cinema,[2] from two in the afternoon until closing time, watching Julie Christie on the screen (endangering his coccyx, but beauty demands its sacrifice). Up there she might be terrorized in a bad film, but she is safe from the passing of time, from vulgar flab, from cancer and the neutron bomb.

He longs to save her from these dangers, just as he longs to save her from that diabolical monster, tenacious and invisible, who ambushes and assults her several times a day. Now Miss Christie is on tenterhooks. She is frightened, and yet, there is nothing in that laboratory where she works that should scare her. All the same, her nostrils (delicious and fragile as a butterfly's wings) quiver almost imperceptibly, and her timid doe-eyes search among the bottles, the jars and the crystal tubes, watchful of the danger which awaits her. "The dictator is unseen yet ever present," Vercingetorix observes. The monster has secured the windows and the doors; when she hears the last bolt being shot, Julie Christie throws herself against the door and screams. Nobody hears her. Now Ecks begins to sweat. He sweats for those beautiful eyes fluttering in terror like a caged bird, for that blond hair ruffled and disorderly, for those soft lips and rounded arms, those avocado breasts and those legs which can no longer assist her to escape. Abruptly Vercingetorix says, "I can't take any more, I'm off."

The cinema is now empty. Alone, Ecks admires the woman's face, larger than life, above him. He is waiting (every minute multiplies the details and prolongs that perverse pleasure) for the machine, irresistible in its pitiless, mechanical fury, to assault the beautiful Julie Christie. The machine begins to shake like the ground in the grip of an earthquake, like a volcano in eruption. Panting, alone, Ecks hears his own breathing amplified in the whirring and grinding of that monster out of control. He is afraid lest his own fantasies will be projected on the screen. He is torn between the secret evil joy that consumes him at the thought of what is soon to happen, and his opposing desire to protect the woman he loves. Implacable, breathing heavily, the machine smashes the objects in the room and pushes aside all obstacles which she hopelessly puts in its way. It laughs as it rips the woman's dress into shreds, and now she stands naked, vulnerable, more beautiful than ever. Naked, Julie Christie does not look naked; she still wears the misty and ambiguous look of her sea-blue eyes, as she is flattened under the thundering machine, amidst a rainbow of laser beams.

Everything around Ecks seems insignificant, but for that act on the screen, polymorphic and enormous, that second rape of Leda by the swan; everything seems irremediably insignificant, in the face of the macrocosmic impact of that orgasm—most insignificant of all those silly, blind little men who have been cowardly enough to leave Julie Christie alone in the laboratory with the machine.

Outside it was raining; a women's group had hung their poster on a public building by the cinema: MAN IS WOMAN'S PAST. When the man behind the counter saw Ecks coming out to buy yet another ticket, he looked ironically at him and said, "You should become a member, like in a football club."

Back in his seat, still inebriated with neon lights and the mist in Julie Christie's blue eyes, Julie Christie kidnapped, impaled by the phallic machine, Ecks was no longer seeing the spectacle on the screen, but only the actress shaking her hair, trembling, whispering *man is woman's past*—a dark unconscious past, deplorable like all pasts. The machine rapes her for the second time, a brutish omnipresent mechanism, impossible to identify because it is in fact a symbol, against which Julie Christie, man's future, can do nothing, for it is massive, coarse, enraged and its enraged obscenity knows no limits: a phallic structure of unlimited power.

After the last show, Ecks came out exhausted, under

18

the amused gaze of the commissionaire.

"I can sell you a still," the man said, with that obtuse sense of superiority of those who don't understand.

"Which one would you like?" he seemed almost paternal. "The rape? We're closing now, but come back tomorrow. Don't worry," he added mockingly, "no problem with seats."

"There are two things I hate in life," answered Ecks. "The second is having to wait."

Vercingetorix was waiting for him, half-drunk near the entrance to the bar. He was standing under the poster, hitting it with his great orangoutang's fists. Though wet, the poster resisted; all the same Vercingetorix had managed to perforate the M of MEN and the S of PAST.

"What are you doing?" Ecks asked him reproachfully. Covered with shreds of letters, a paperclown, Vercingetorix answered, "I'm tearing man's future to pieces." He spoke with the quickness of a drunkard accustomed to rescuing his words from drowning in wine.

1. Ecks thought that names were irrelevant, as was gender, although in both cases people did their best to live up to them. Once he had amused himself writing down a list of possible names. Ulysses sounded right, alluding to his condition of traveller, but its literary resonance was limiting. He would have felt obliged to re-write the *Odyssey* in modern terms: any excuse to keep one away from a self-sacrificing wife. He would have also liked to be called Ivan, but he was sure that somebody would think of him as a refugee from behind the Iron Curtain. And as for Humbert, it was impossible after the publication of *Lolita*. Archibald was imposing, but

old-fashioned. Had he been a knight of some order? He would have to check that in an encyclopaedia. His neighbour had just bought a brand-new edition of 36 volumes whose red covers matched the leather of her armchairs. With it she had been given a little varnished table on which she had placed the television and the cat.

Ecks knew a man whose occupation was to sell encyclopaedias in installments. He was acquainted with all the excuses that delinquent subscribers can give and had published them in a leaflet which had received a prize from the Association of Door-to-door Salesmen. Ecks had met him by accident. The salesman had tried to sell him installments of a *Practical History of Medicine*. In confidence he had told Ecks that almost all his clients were hypochondriacs. "Like me," Ecks answered. "If you buy them all at once," suggested the salesman; "you'll be able to give yourself rapid and efficient diagnoses without spending money on doctors."

"I prefer to buy them every Monday when they come out," insisted Ecks. "By the end of the week I always feel worse and by Sunday I'll take to bed with definite expectations, sure that I shall discover the name of my latest illness in the following installment."

The salesman had seemed somewhat perplexed. He took out his notebook and began to write. "Repeat that bit about your *expectations*," he urged. He read over his notes to make sure that they were correct. "Extraordinary," he said. "Nobody has used this argument before. I shall put it in my new edition of *Advice for Door-to-door Salesmen*. Dear me, you learn something new every day. When I come up with an answer, I'll call you." Meanwhile he had bought Ecks a beer.

2. As a consequence of inflation and videos, they pulled down the theatre and made its site an auto graveyard, a place no less dilapidated than the old building. Years later—by now Julie Christie had evaded the monster and become a novice in a convent of barefoot nuns—Ecks discovered in the nearby yard a piece of the cinema's neon sign: it was the X of Rex, a few bulbs and wires still attached. There was no chance of ever lighting it, but Ecks hugged it to him, not without some resentment, and dragged it all the way home. Rasping with the strain, he took it up the stairs. The landlady made no objection. He presumed she was tired of seeing him living alone. A dead letter was preferable to a barking dog.

The Journey, IV: The Story of Ecks

Soon after arriving in a city, Ecks finds work—he is flexible and can earn his living in many ways: teaching German romanticism, sweeping the platforms of the metro, as stenographer in a maritime transport company or waiting on tables.[1]

He then rents a room, buys some books (Ecks is resigned to buying the same books in different cities), a few records (he adores Wagner and his days are much happier when he can listen to Kirsten Flagstad singing *O sink hernieder*) and installs one or two objects, valueless but for their sentimental associations. They are not always the same, because Ecks has learned that his existence, like that of most people, is a ceaseless exchange of losses and acquisitions. Through chance, accident or forgetfulness, we often lose those things we love, and purchase—by mistake or indifference—objects that we never wanted to possess.

Going from city to city, Ecks has acquired some things and lost others. Often he wakes up suddenly from dreams with a strong desire to hold again an object long since left behind in a hotel bedroom or given away, and thus knows how intense this desire can be, as if his physical and moral well-being depended upon it. Yet he can still claim that he accepts the passing of material things, their disappearance, as a natural phenomenon, immersed as he is in the flow of time, like a fish in the current of the river. Perhaps for the same reason, he does not experience excessive joy when, having moved to some other place, a lost article comes back into his possession.

1. It is not true that Ecks has always found it easy to obtain employment in the cities where he has lived during his long and inconclusive odyssey. These are difficult times and people suspect a stranger. Those who live always in the same place—the countrymen or city-dwellers who only travel on holiday or for family reasons—do not realize that to be a stranger is a temporary situation, one that can be altered; in fact they assume that some men *are* strangers and others not. They believe that one is born—and does not become—a stranger.

Once walking through the streets of a foreign city, Ecks met a young woman who looked like someone he had known elsewhere in the past. It could be that the resemblance was more illusory than real—having travelled a lot, Ecks is familiar with the phenomenon of *déjà vu*, believing it to be an hallucination, shadows of nostalgia and loneliness. All the same, with an ambiguity of emotions, Ecks approached and politely invited her to have coffee with him.

"Excuse me," he said in an accent which she could not fail to recognize as foreign. "You remind me of someone I used to know long ago. Do not feel offended by this, but would you come to a café with me?"

More surprised than intrigued, the girl had not refused the unusual invitation. They sat at a red table in an awful American bar to which Ecks took an immediate dislike. She had chosen it, and he felt it would be discourteous to object. The music was loud and the place was full of slot machines. The air smelled of fat and sweat, and the walls were covered with glittering photographs of hot dogs with French fries. She asked for a vanilla ice cream topped with whipped cream and chocolate. Ecks ordered a coffee.

"Are you a foreigner?" She inquired as if that had great importance. Ecks was annoyed.

"Only in some countries," he answered, "and hopefully, I will not be one forever."

She looked at him with surprise.

"I was not born a foreigner," he explained. "It is a condition one acquires through force of circumstances. You could become one too, if you chose, though I don't advise it. Not on a permanent basis."

Two out of three men who approach me are mad, she thought, blaming her poor luck. She was not bad-looking, had done two years at university and there were no noticeable defects in her family. Somewhere she had read that human beings, like animals, release a chemical odour, apparently inperceptible but operating as a powerful source of attraction or repulsion. Without doubt hers attracted madmen...and the world was full of them. Such men could not all be put into madhouses; there were too many of them. Indeed many were apparently normal until that particular odour triggered derangement. Though these less dangerous madmen were allowed to roam loose, they should be obliged to wear a sign, a badge— like people with special allergies—to stop others having to deal with them as if they were sane.

"It was years ago," Ecks said, "when I met the

24

woman who resembles you so much, if you will forgive the comparison."

His style of speech was rhetorical and somewhat archaic. She thought that it was because foreigners learned to speak a language in an artificial way; or perhaps it was all part of his madness.

"It was years ago," insisted Ecks. "I was only six."

All that was needed now, she thought, was for him to start telling her about his childhood. Madmen always go back over their childhood. Could she possibly get up and go without provoking a scene?

"It was all rather strange: she was a foreigner and perhaps that's why I fell in love with her."

"At the age of six?" the girl asked, alarmed.

"It was my first love," Ecks answered, not without a certain pride which instantly he regretted. Why feel proud of it?

"What really matters," he stressed, "is that she was a foreigner."

The girl stared at him.

"Don't you see?" added Ecks. "She was tall and slender with chestnut hair, and she spoke our language with difficulty. For me, at the age of six, the sounds of her *r* and her sibilant *z* were a source of great delight."

He's completely mad, the girl told herself. How can I get out of this? I could say "They're expecting me at work," or make a dash through the back door. One never knows how a madman will react.

Suddenly Ecks felt melancholic; he wondered whether he should continue with his story or not.

"And you, how many foreigners have you met?"

Now she had missed her chance. She should have got up and run the moment he had fallen silent. Running

25

out did not matter. Besides, it was getting late.

Her silence increased his melancholia.

"The other day I saw an old woman in the metro," he began suddenly. "She was sitting in front of me. I must add that she was lovely, with white hair and a youthful smile; her eyes were vivacious and seemed to smile also. She was looking around curiously and with evident pleasure. She was holding a bag with fruit or vegetables; it seemed rather heavy. She smiled directly at me and I was deeply moved. But then, the emotions of an immigrant are rather unstable."

That's it, she thought, now he's going to tell me his clinical history, how he escaped from the hospital, and I'll have to call the police. How I hate getting involved with other people's problems...

"We become oversensitive," said Ecks. "I was reminded of an aunt of mine, an old aunt who used to knit me pullovers when I was little and bake me currant buns. I've not seen her for years. I began to look at the old dear as if she were my aunt, and I felt such tenderness that my eyes filled with tears. I wanted to show her my affection, help her up her stairs, make her some soup and listen with her to the radio. I wanted to talk to her of summer and winter, of the taste of tomatoes and lettuce, of the price of sugar and of the decadence of today's values. You won't believe it, but this woman looking at me so tenderly was reaching beyond my silence, becoming involved in my thoughts. Don't you think that there is nothing like human involvement? There we were, facing each other in the compartment of an underground train which was hissing like an asthmatic, feeling a deep involvement with each other. She was smiling whimsically over the oranges and garlic in her bag. I was smiling back, and an exchange of harmony and cordiality flowed between us. When the train stopped at my station, I did not think of getting off, I did not mind where I ended up, because I was travelling with my aunt, in an aroma of lemons and baking, half-a-dozen ripe figs lying in her skirt, so carefully pressed. We were in no hurry, but continued to smile at each other in the shadows of the compartment, not noticing the bad smell or the dirty and stiffling atmosphere. She offered me half an apple (which she cut with a pocket knife) and I ate it.''

Perhaps he's a pervert with a fetish for old women, the girl thought. This would spare me certain complications. I may look like someone he met as a child, but no way can he take me for old.

"When she got off," continued Ecks, "I followed her. I offered to carry her shopping bag. She answered with that radiant smile. Do you understand what I mean by 'radiant'?''

Besides being a foreigner he presumed to know her language better than she did, and seemed ready to teach her. This was too much.

"Of course I do," she answered with irritation.

"She gave me the bag and we walked to the door of her house. She asked me in. I wanted to weep.''

Do madmen weep? She wasn't sure. Perhaps they did.

"I was going to accept her invitation, but I turned it down. I feared that if I entered her house I would never want to leave.''

She noticed that he was looking far away, possibly recalling the scene, and took the advantage to escape.

The Journey, V: The Story of Ecks

After nine years of never-ending travel (it was more in the nature of a flight than a journey), Ecks arrived at the city of A. where he found work in the zoo; his duties were to hose down the cages.[1] He rented an attic in the old part of the city near the port. He actually rather resented the word "attic" for its associations with nineteenth-century novels, Argentinian *tangos*, unwed mothers, eternal students, people affected by skin disease, and drunks. All the same, his salary from the zoo did not run to anything better than a hated attic: his earnings would not not have kept either a chimpanzee or a polar bear in food for a week. But then in this, as in most cases, it was quality that counted, and when Ecks compared himself to a polar bear—there was a very attractive specimen at the zoo with whom he was on most cordial terms—he had to admit that the bear, belonging to a threatened species, deserved more attention. He, a mere human, belonged to a species over crowded, predatory, and in constant growth—like rats.

Ecks arrived at A. in the month of May. Which, as he well knew, signifies nothing unless we specify the hemisphere, since, as a result of the delicate balance of the planets, in some cities it will be spring while in others autumn, just as some countries are at war when others are at peace.

In the city of A. during the month of May, the chestnuts are in flower; the plane trees along the avenues spew unpleasant yellow filaments which, weightless, float in the air and irritate the eyes of passersby. The ice cream sellers are out in force and children play truant from school; the old and suffocating underground trains fill with heat and rancid smells. In spring the zoo is crowded; hibernating animals wake, yawning and stretching their gaunt limbs. It is now that those undergraduates who have completed their academic year return to their families in the provinces, and attics become vacant.

List of Objects which Ecks provisionally installed in the attic of the city of A.

There was a single shelf (of shiny varnished wood) on which Ecks placed:

A roosting dove of painted blue clay, adorned with a bright pink rose. The dove, with its spread wings and yellow beak, made Ecks feel peaceful. Somewhere, real doves, plump, content with the world and themselves, were hatching their eggs. Ecks couldn't remember how he had come into possession of the dove, but he liked its shape and caressed with pleasure its smooth surface.

An engraving of Venice, which he thought to be a reproduction of a canvas by Canaletto, or perhaps Vanvitelli; he was not sure, sometimes his memory played him tricks, to the extent that he could effortlessly remember a picture not yet painted.[2] On the delicate copper—whose indefinite colouring midway between rose and amber reminded Ecks of Venetian sunsets from the Giudecca—was etched one of those palaces originally belonging to rich merchants who trafficked in gold and crystal. By the side of the palace floated two or three slender boats without sails used for the transport of water-barrels, and a larger one from whose mast hung the loop of a tied-up sail.

In this small and seductive image Ecks found solace. The harmony of the buildings and the symmetry of the canals suggested the existence of a possible order and equilibrium which redeemed so much else.

On the shelf there was also an old tin of Hornimans Tea which Ecks had found hidden at the bottom of a cupboard. Beneath the red lettering edged with gold lacquer the word *Boudoir* was written in italics. What gave Ecks the most satisfaction, however, was the picture: on the black surface the unknown artist—an Englishman, Ecks supposed—had outlined an oval vignette of a girl reclining on a red *chaise-longue*, reading a book. On the corner of the table at her side stood a vase of flowers and a teapot. There were more flowers peeping through the window above her. At the bottom of the tin there was a second vignette within an oval frame of another girl wearing a bonnet, languidly seated on a sofa—Ecks could easily make out its pattern of red flowers—with two little cushions, one scarlet, one rose, beside her. The white curtains were bordered with lilac frills, and behind the sofa stood a lamp, its shade hung with a green fringe. The girl's hand was raised to bring the white porcelain cup to her lips. The same scene was repeated on the other side of the Hornimans tin with small variations—the girl's dress was black with a V neckline, its short sleeves ending in green bows; at her feet lay a dazzling white cushion.

Sometimes in his imagination Ecks blended the two girls, the unread books, the unfading flowers, as in a mixture of tea leaves. In moments of frustration or loneliness Ecks thought he would like to be that girl who contentedly read her book while sipping tea.

He also amused himself imagining the titles of the books the girl might be reading—*Persuasion*, *The Vicar of Wake field*, Pushkin's *The Captain's Daughter*, *Middlemarch*, *Silas Marner*—though sometimes he preferred to think she was turning the pages of some work not yet written, imaginary, perverse.

The books which Ecks buys as soon as he arrives and settles in a new place are almost always the same: *The Bible, The Odyssey, The Aeneid, Robinson Crusoe*, *Gulliver's Travels*, Poe's stories, Kafka's *Trial* and *Metamorphosis*, the lyrics of Catullus and Shakespeare's *Sonnets*.[3] And of course an old dictionary with notches and gilding at the side, among whose pages Ecks searches for the pen drawings of birds with hooked beaks (like the goshawk), for the yak and orix, and the faded reproduction of the shield of Breslau.

Ecks also likes to look at the atlases in these old editions, with their gazetteers of ancient geography, their maps with countries that no longer exist and cities that have changed names. As after a long tyranny, the tyrant once dead and his rule broken, all visible traces disappear from the cities (street names, busts, monuments) and other names, other monuments replace them, so in dictionaries new words appear as others vanish, new meanings flourish and the maps are changing. Ecks finds pleasure too in the drawings of mythical beasts imagined by men, in which the shape of the lion blends with that of the raven, woman with fish, bat with crocodile, or the little unicorn which Magdalena Strozzi cradles in her arms in Raphael's famous painting.[4]

1. In his conversation and travel notes Ecks deliberately avoids naming the city of A. and other cities, apparently to escape offending anybody's susceptibilities. Virgil and Dante, to give only two examples, paid dear for their lack of discretion on this point. The mood of cities varies considerably; today they sanctify what yesterday they crushed. They suffer from shortness of memory, and sulfuric acid (not to mention lead pollution and other effluents) corrodes their nerves worse than herpes.

The fact is, Ecks detests any city which is not by the sea. By contrast he adores ports, their soot-blackened buildings, smeared walls, wet newspapers in the gutters, dead birds and paper cartons among the refuse. Though it is intended that the cities here should be surrounded by an aura of mystery, the reader is invited to play a game to entertain himself during the rainy spells. On the basis of the hints given in the course of the novel, the reader must guess the identity of those cities alluded to. (Our age has produced few original games—wars, for example, are not unique to our time——and has displayed in this area considerable lack of wit and imagination. Most of our entertainment comes from the past, even though complemented now by sophisticated additions, such as guided missiles, joysticks, magnetic tapes and microchips). What we read about the city of A., for example, is that in the month of May the chestnuts flower and the plane trees irritate passersby. This means that we can immediately eliminate Paris on the grounds that it is not a port, London because it has no plane trees, Santiago de Campostela, though full of students and attics, for not being on the sea. And so on.

Unlike *Don Quixote*, whose author also fails to reveal the birthplace of his hero, it is almost impossible to trace the stages of Ecks' journey on any map. By contrast, it is quite common even for those who have not read Cervantes to follow the route of Don Quixote—it figures in almost all the itineraries set out by the tourist agencies. (Frankly, it's not worth the bother: dust, mediocre food, hardly a windmill in sight, let alone giants. On the other hand, I recommend another literary itinerary, the one travelled by the gentleman with his enchanting Lolita. The route is better, the landscape more varied, and a lot goes on by the side of the road.)

If, dear reader, your deductions lead you to guess that Ecks spent some time in the following cities: Old York, Merlin, Stretch Jersey, Texaco, Ombu-Beach, Psycho-Aires, Asnapolis, Megalopolis, Kreutzer-Sonata, Anagram and Quac-quac, you have won the "stateless citizen" certificate, inconvenient at borders, but very useful for writing poetry.

2. The best way for a foreigner to get to know a city is to fall in love with one of its women, someone inclined to mother a man far from home and also appreciative of different pigmentation. She will trace him a path that does not figure on any map and instruct him in a language he will never forget. She will show the stranger the bridges and the secret corners of the place, and, nurturing him like a babe, teach him to lisp his first words, take his first steps, and recite the names of birds and trees. Actually, I am not quite sure about this last point: in the big cities where we live the names of birds and trees are no longer familiar, and anyway, for all the notice we take of them, the trees could be made of plastic, like the tablecloths.

In his dreams Ecks has made love to unknown women, returned to his childhood and completed unfinished tasks, he has seen revolving mountains and motionless rivers, has been pursued by armies of different nations—all looking alike—has suffered catastrophies for the slightest of sins and has painted numerous pictures which nobody has yet seen. In dreams he displays feverish energy, performs ceaseless tasks upon which so much depends. He could never paint those pictures in his waking life: he lacks the aptitude and the necessary technique. All the same, he tries to keep them hung in his memory, as in a private gallery, where he also displays the clandestine lovers of his dreams, emerging from the cloisters of the night. He could start a museum with those canvases, those women. But nothing is more private than dreams and their privacy is an ambivalent gift.

The Laws of Hospitality

Once, for courtesy, I loved a stranger.
(A reversible condition, this strangeness,
I too was a stranger for her.)
Her tongue, which stung like an asp,
was not the same as mine;
and I, out of courtesy,
let hers come first.
At the letter *a* our love began,
I spelled out for her the old romances,
and sounded out the word *approximate*.
My "i's" surprised her,
as did the colour of our seas;
I found her "s's" much too strong
and wondered at the names of her streets.
Her tongue was eager,
but scarcely flexible
and I vainly looked for equivalents

34

of "I love you", "I long for the touch of your hand".
Like the blind, we had to love each other
in different codes
and I was not always sure
that she understood what I meant.
I wished to give her this city—
its long streets and grey skies—
I wanted to sing her lullabies
to ease her loneliness.
I wanted to build her a house of brand-new words
with musical doors
and secret seals.
I longed to be lover and brother.
Ancient laws for welcoming the stranger
led me to be courteous and fair:
The first taste of banquets
went to her
and the whitest of sheets.
When she left
I was alone,
This tongue of mine was mine no longer.
I stammered strange words,
wandered through the outskirts
of an empty city
and in this hospitality
I lost my name.

3. There follows another list of books. These were
ordered by Ecks from a bookshop in the mystery city,
but we do not know if he ever received them—his relations with the shopkeepers of this town left much to be
desired. One bookshop was only up to selling postcards
of Mount Carmel in winter, with snow like icing on a

cake, subscriptions to fashion magazines, horoscopes, knick-knacks, and green balls of low-quality *hashish*, which the secondary school students would chew like gum. Here is the list:

The Garden of Forking Desires, by George Lewis Barges. (Blindness sharpens one's literary sense, as does childhood deafness. He who lacks the ability to notice the appearance of things is capable of much keener memory and imagination, just as those who learn to speak late will always feel more at home with the written word. According to his mother, Ecks learnt to speak at the age of three after great cajoling by his family and neighbours. The first word he said was: "No". Everybody began to cry with joy because they had begun to fear he would remain mute; but he, confused and upset by the tears and thinking he might have hurt someone, felt guilty and said: "Yes". Since then he has had great problems with negatives, for fear of causing offense. He can only say *no* in his dreams and even then he regrets it.)

A Fool and His Fire by Dieu La Rochelle. ("Do you feel anxiety sometimes?" asked the doctor. "No," Ecks replied, "always.")

The Hydrangeas by Felisberto Hernandez. (Ecks is obsessive about flowers, but only acacias, and not at all about dolls. On the other hand his friend Vercingetorix has a special attraction to female dwarfs, especially those who work in the circus. Besides, he owns a curious collection of twenty-five porcelain statuettes of girls in those knee-length bathing costumes from the old days. He acquired them as a result of complicated international exchanges—Vercingetorix would never pay money for his trophies, his taste and personality belong to the age

36

before the dollar was king. The twenty-five miniature bathers (which, like a jealous lover, he will not show to anybody) hold the most ingenious positions which, Ecks thinks, must approach pure deviance. One stretches out a thin and delicate arm, and points with long fingers towards a far-away or non-existent sea; another tucks a yellow curl beneath the rim of her bathing cap; there is another whose delicately poised toes are on the point of kicking a ball, and a fourth who carelessly adjusts the buckle of her shoe. Ecks asked Vercingetorix if this collection provoked some kind of erotic excitement in him and Vercingetorix—a broad, tall and robust man, somewhat uncouth—angrily replied: "Of course not. It's aesthetic, even metaphysical.")

The Death of a Chinese Checquer Player by Akira Kusawata. (Please note: This is not a thriller written under a pseudonym by Bioy Casares, as might be assumed. Ecks prided himself on avoiding reading even one of these throughout his life. The Hoggarth Press catalogue for 1969 gives a brief reference to Kusawata's book: it is a 98-page novel-in-verse describing every sequence of a game which took place in the thirteenth century between the Emperor Tiu-Kiu and his lieutenant. They were playing for their souls and, at the Emperor's defeat, his rival took possession of the loser's dreams, memories and ambitions, while retaining his own dreams and desires. The ambiguity of his situation drove the lieutenant mad, for he did not know whether he had loved or killed in his own name or in that of the Emperor, and he found himself knowing more things than his mind could support. He ended up killing himself by committing *harakiri*.)

Women and Utopias by César Moro. (A description

of fantastic fauna: singing machines, the monstrous two-faced *Anfisbena*, characters out of paintings or fables, all of female gender.)

4. The fact that the unicorn frequently appears in the company of domestic animals (dogs, cats, rabbits, goats) in medieval tapestries and in the paintings of the more famous schools, makes one suspect that it was not just a mythical beast. Why should Raphael, for example, in his portrait of Magdalena Strozzi (whose serene and earthly beauty is devoid of weakness), set a fantastical creature in her arms? Nothing else is imaginary in Raphael's painting, neither the columns which frame the canvas, nor the pale Roman countryside with its mist-shrouded hills. The golden pendant which hangs on the smoothly corsetted breasts of Magdalena Strozzi is executed to perfection. There is not a superfluous brush stroke in the painting; neither the curve of that smooth forehead nor the timid shadow beneath the chin suggest any hint of fantasy. Why then should the small and tender unicorn, whose open mouth seems to invite all caresses, be the only unreal element in the canvas? Would it be too far-fetched to believe that unicorns existed, perhaps as pets and companions for women? (After all, the great polemic which took place in the XV century in Flanders was only concerned with how many legs the unicorn possessed, not with its existence.)

The Journey, VI: Some People Ecks Met In His Travels

On the Italian cruise ship Ecks once met a certain Joseph L., a musician who earned his living playing the piano in nightclubs. Ecks asked him to play *As Time Goes By* (Ingrid Bergman was the second love of his life, though she never acknowledged this). Joseph L. said he did not know it. Instead he played *The Falling Leaves*. Ecks felt that indeed there was little difference between the passage of time and falling leaves—Homer must have been the first to point this out. Ecks invited Joseph L. to have a brandy with him. In those days the musician was in his mid-forties (a rather tricky age for emigrating, he admitted) and had been recently operated on for a stomach ulcer caused—he assumed—by the excessive amount of smoke present in the clubs where he worked; even though he did not smoke, he was obliged to inhale the poison of other people's cigarettes. He doubted very much whether he ever would be able to adjust to living in another country, but Ecks tried to reassure him by saying that places were like pianos: one had to get used to playing them, lightly at first, starting with just a few chords, until their best notes became evident.

Ecks met Joseph L. again years later (he did not know how many; all this travelling disrupted his sense of time until it seemed like a piece of elastic, now stretching infinitely, now crisp, tight and full of knots). Joseph L. no longer played the piano, he ran a five-star hotel on a well-known tourist island, smoked perfumed Havanas, and was fluent in several languages. He invited Ecks to have a whiskey with him. When they parted, Joseph L. asked Ecks to hum *As Time Goes By*, but by then Ecks had forgotten it. He only remembered *The Falling Leaves*.

In another place it was the run-down lower quarters of the city that Ecks loved to wander. He loved the Chinese lanterns and coloured-paper chains hung there to attract sailors from the Dutch and Filipino ships anchored nearby. Here he once met a fat, good-natured man whose lower lip had been split by a bullet. He was in love with a very young girl, alone and the mother of a black child. This character owned and ran a small bar whose walls were entirely covered with photographs of race horses and jockeys, for when he was young he had been a great fan of horse racing. Before he fell in love, he used to send out his last customers at midnight on the dot. But one day the girl came into his bar, sat at one of those round tables with wrought iron legs and marble tops near the window and, looking first at her little dark-skinned daughter and then at him—he was standing respectfully by her side waiting to serve her—asked for a Coca-Cola and two glasses. From that day he kept the bar open all night in the hope that the young mother and her daughter, sleepy and tired, would return. He was suffering from insomnia anyway—he would explain—and if they were to come again, he wouldn't want them to find the bar closed. Nothing worse than a city at night with its billboards lighting up only hostile houses and closed bars. The girl had in fact come back a couple of times, always with the child to whom he gave raspberry candies, a gold medal which he had worn around his neck since childhood, a collection of old coins in a coffee tin, and a storybook. He had not dared give anything to the young mother for fear of offending her, but they had chatted of this and that. On being asked what "this and that" consisted of, the fat man had replied—loneliness, life, death, the price of cooking oil and gasoline, primary schools and childhood illnesses.

When Ecks came back to this city, he looked for the bar and it was there. That comforted him: it hurt him to return to places and discover that so much had changed. Ecks felt change was a deep betrayal, a blow almost physical. But the bar was still there, open day and night (it is difficult to cure insomnia) and the fat man was still serving, good-natured and polite as ever. He recognized Ecks and when after a while Ecks asked him for news of the girl and her little black daughter, he cleared his throat a bit (a slight cold he'd caught the night before staying up to wash bottles and count the till) and said that she still came every once in a while to sit at her usual table with a Coke and two glasses. She would stay a while and they would talk of this and that.

A story without progress, but then again the two men agreed that the essence of some stories lies precisely in this: they do not change, but remain like citadels or lighthouses facing the irresistible assault of time.

The Journey, VII: Ecks and Dreams

Whenever he wakes in a bad mood, he knows it is because he has had some revelation in his dreams, one so powerful and unbearable it is better forgotten. Like all revelations, those which come in dreams are given to people unable to understand them, much less act on them. For in dreams one is always naïve, inadequate and lacking discernment. Therefore one either forgets or ignores their content.

But the sense of guilt which comes from rejecting the sibylline teaching of dreams puts Ecks in a bad mood. He feels like the apostle Peter, burdened with a command whose message has no place in the simple life of a Hebrew fisherman.

When we sleep we are all simple fishermen, until a sudden light puts us on the road to wisdom. "This is the path," the dream tells us, "follow its guide." But on waking we turn down the offer out of laziness or resignation, or on the pretext that we have to hurry after today's catch or be our brother's keeper. We return to our old ways, thinking of Peter.

Sometimes Ecks dreams of fishing in water so clear that he can see and follow to the very bottom the fishes' comings and goings. He can also exist in this water without having to swim, without getting wet, without drowning, as though he were moving in air. Dreams have their own logic; only in the ambiguity of daylight do we need to reason and compare, to pin down the weft of things. Dreams are so persuasive, they need no argument. (Nothing could be less rhetorical than a dream.)

The tackle that Ecks carries in his dream is extravagant and heavy. Yet a feeling of happiness prevails. In the transparent water he watches the profusion of fishes, big and small, the shells, molluscs and all the sea fauna and flora, brilliant and inviting. Since Ecks has this dream quite often, he knows from the start that out on the beach there will be a tall house of grey stone with a balcony overlooking the sea. When the tide is high, it will be difficult to reach the house, for the waves invade the path with leads to its door. Fishing is slow with the heavy tackle Ecks uses, and when it is time to go to the house he always has a sense of impending danger. He now discovers that the water has reached the balcony and that the waves are crushing him against the walls. He can't go back, because behind him the tide has flooded the whole beach. Nor can he go forward. There is only one spot where he can stand—a small outcrop below the main wall—beneath which the water rolls, very blue, very dense. To add to the anguish of his situation, he is aware that the tackle on his back is bearing down on him, but he can't get loose from it. It has become trapped in the rock.

Despite this, Ecks awakes with the sensation that the adventure and the fishing have been pleasant. So pleasant, in fact, that he suspects the dream was not about fishing, but something else.

The Journey, VIII: The Ship of Fools

In the painting the ship has already sailed. On board, men in evening dress, starched collars, white gloves and shiny patent-leather shoes, are dressed as for a party. They have embarked wearing the finery and solemn expressions used on big occasions. Far out to sea, a few lights are shining.

The old story goes that ships loaded with lunatics were taken out to sea, where the water was deepest and troubled by strong currents. Once there, the sailors would quietly leave by smaller boats and, abandoning the passengers to their fate, return to shore. The madmen would hardly notice, or if they made any objection at being left alone on board, they were easily reassured that the crew would only be away for a short while, to obtain provisions and fresh drinking water or to see to some essential repairs. There is no record of a rebellion ever having taking place, perhaps because of the discipline exercised on board, perhaps because the rocking motion of the sea rendered them docile.

There remains an anecdote told by a certain Artemius Gudröm, one of the few sailors involved to keep a record of this barbarous practice. Artemius, a naval engineer of some fame in the sixteenth century, was also a gambler and, having got heavily into debt, was imprisoned in a jail in Renania. Unable to bear prison any longer, he agreed, in order to gain remittance of his sentence, to serve under a false name as captain of one of these ships. According to the journal he left—*Ars navigatoris*—he undertook three such journeys to complete his sentence. His account is not detailed; perhaps he was not keen to remember the episodes, or perhaps he was too involved in the technical aspects of navigation: depth and draught of the vessel, measurements of the keel, types of sails, etc.

Artemius tells that, in the year 1583, a ship under his charge set sail from a port in Flanders. The voyage proved uneventful, as anticipated, until the ship came within sight of the coast of Lovaina. On board were 36 lunatics, mostly from various towns of Renania, of whom 22 were men, ten were women and the remaining four, children verging on adolescence. Besides Artemius, the crew consisted of eight ex-prisoners from jails in Saxonia, who had signed on for much the same reasons as himself.

Water and provisions were beginning to run short, but Artemius was not worried, for he and his eight men would soon desert the ship and return safely to shore. One of the lunatics, however, whom Artemius calls Glaucus Torrender, showed signs of unrest and had done so almost from the beginning of the trip.

Though the rocking of the sea (a motion which Artemius curiously describes in three different ways) had a hypnotic effect on most passengers, some of whom, after contemplating the water for a while with heads tilted forward, were on the point of falling into it—some indeed had fallen without anybody making any attempt to save them—this phenomenon did not seem to occur in the case of Glaucus Torrender; on the contrary the rocking seemed to cause him greater agitation. Artemius observes at this point that Glaucus was not an ordinary madman. Intelligent, alert and perceptive, Glaucus had been conspicuous from the very first day for his sense of order and responsibility. He had not only shown an interest in the art of navigation, easily learning how to control and steer the ship, but he had also taken charge of the distribution of food, the rationing of water and the supply of salt.

Artemius states that Glaucus was a splendid administrator and that his help during the journey had been essential, particularly since the rest of the crew were nothing but drunkards, unruly and quarrelsome. One assumes that the two men became friends, as much as a half-madman, seemingly sane, and a half-sane man, seemingly mad, can ever be. From Artemius's report we gather that he did not often converse with Glaucus: their friendship developed in silence, as they shared their tasks. We also gather that the latter was not prey to fits of delirium, as were the other madmen, nor to those delusions or confusion of identities which can afflict the insane.

Glaucus's only symptom was a pernicious insomnia which kept him awake on deck, when everyone but the helmsman was asleep. Glaucus did not sleep a single night, nor did he show any signs of tiredness or need to sleep during the day. While the other passengers, lulled by the rolling of the sea, entered into a state of deep hypnosis, or into fits, deliriously assuming that they were somewhere else, holding imaginary conversations or proclaiming eccentric soliloquies, Glaucus attended to the ship's course, distributed provisions—ever watchful against attempts to steal them—and studied the position of the stars. Was he at all aware of the end of this strange voyage?

The day came when it was time for the crew to

abandon both ship and passengers to their fate. Artemius had anticipated the possibility that Glaucus would stay awake that night, prey to his habitual restlessness, and that he might put up some resistance at the sight of the crew preparing to cast off in the dinghy. For this reason he had prepared in advance a generous sleeping potion, (made with herbs from India) sufficient to put a horse to sleep. But when he came to look for it among his belongings, the draught had disappeared. Disconcerted by its loss, deprived of the remedy on which he had been counting, he even considered taking Glaucus along, but he feared the reaction of his unsympathetic, rascally crew. Besides, his sentence was not yet commuted, and such a breach of discipline might well put him back into that prison he so dreaded.

As the moment of leaving drew near, Artemius verified that all the lunatics were asleep. As usual, Glaucus was on deck, sitting on a barrel, apparently calm, though watchful, his eyes following the captain's every movement. Artemius records that a waning moon shone over the stormy sea; low clouds swooped above the water like shadows of fleeing birds.

The crew was becoming impatient; already they had untied the boat. Uneasily, Artemius took his leave of Glaucus. Convinced of the man's partial lunacy, he explained that he and his crew had decided to sail to the nearest stretch of coast to obtain provisions. Knowing as he did of Glaucus' competency, he was leaving him in charge of the ship. He was to circle slowly, without stopping, until they returned with dry biscuits, salted meat, butter and cheese. Artemius recounts that the look which Glaucus gave him was so sad and full of terror that it gave him the shivers and he only just managed to spit out the last few words.

No sooner had Artemius made his excuses than a blood-curdling scream was heard, followed by loud imprecations and oaths. The lowered boat, upon touching the water, had sunk.

Artemius briefly recounts the events of the following days. He sailed the ship as near as possible to the coast. The madmen, deprived of food, were showing signs of restlessness, and the crew, angered by the loss of their means of escape, had become even more brutal. In spite of Artemius' protests, several lunatics were thrown overboard. Glaucus watched in silence. Once near the coast, Artemius gave orders for everyone to jump into the water and attempt to swim ashore. He knew well that the lunatics, for fear of the sea, would never dare to do so, and even those who might would be too weak to survive in the water for long.

In fact, perhaps because they did not understand his order, or were too deep in dreams where neither shores, rocks, nor even death itself figured, the madmen did not jump. Only Glaucus followed the captain and crew into the water. Soon after, under the yellow moonlight, Artemius saw him drown, shrouded in white foam. In the distance the ship of fools sailed aimlessly on.

(In the painting the anonymous artist depicts the ship with its cargo of mad souls setting out from a port in Flanders. On the esplanade by the sea, a crowd has gathered to watch the spectacle, women with parasols and men with silver-tipped walking sticks. The ladies lift elegant fingers and the men attend to them politely, some talking, others looking out to sea. The painter has given more prominence to the spectators than to the distant ship on whose crowded deck Ecks has sought in vain for wild-eyed Glaucus and the profile of renowned Artemius.)

In this continuous wandering from city to city the thing which most troubles Ecks is the impossibility of keeping a dog. He wouldn't want to leave it behind when he goes away, and, on the other hand, it is very expensive to move a dog from one place to another. Besides he does not know whether such an insecure existence would be to a dog's liking, a domesticated animal which so loves its home and its routine. That is also why Ecks keeps neither plants nor wife (another domesticated animal which loves its home and its routine).

The Journey, IX: The Cement Factory

On a bleak, cold August morning Vercingetorix disappeared. He had taken no measures to protect himself nor had he planned to leave. Leaving can become an involuntary act which catches us unexpectedly, just as we innocently postulate infinite time and space ahead. To disappear is no longer voluntary, but acquires passive form: "*We are being disappeared*," Vercingetorix had said on those few occasions when he referred to these things.

Vercingetorix had no time to prepare for his journey, or take leave of his friends, or even say good-bye to the neighbours who had locked all their windows and doors while seven armed men (two chewing gum) took him away under a blanket with bandages over his eyes. He would have liked to say something to the lady next door who washed his clothes and to the man selling papers at the corner who gave him quiet tips on the horses in the Saturday races. But surely he was now in another kind of race, and the frightened lady hid behind her wardrobe, while the newspaper seller softly whistled the "spider" *tango* and looked away.

Meanwhile Vercingetorix was being hit and bundled into a blue car without license plates, nevertheless of a type well known in the city. (So well known that when it appeared, like a dinosaur rearing above the plain, the streets would empty. Men and women fled, windows and doors closed and suddenly no other noise could be heard but the threatening breath of the monster, as it flattened under its claws doorsills, roots of trees and pavements.)

As his arms were being tied behind his back and the dinosaur pissed at length against his hands. Vercingetorix regretted only two things: leaving his blue canary which no one would go and feed—for his room would now be sequestered and eventually become the refuge of some sickly beggar—and missing the opening of the circus, which had appeared a few days earlier and erected its tent in a clearing by the side of the old train station built by the English.

Vercingetorix had gone around there the day before his disappearance: strange how future events serve in retrospect to date those which, apparently insignificant, are part of the past. He had looked at the equipment, the lions and tigers cages; walked among the electric cables lying on the ground like tired lizards, admired the arches of lights which stood against the sky like a row of birds waiting for crumbs, and bought a ticket for the opening night. He did not want to miss the ring-master heralding through the loudspeaker the entrance of those acrobatic twins, capable of death-defying leaps, the Queen of the Elephants, so fragile between the wrinkled ears of the pachyderm, the Russian giant able to sustain on his shoulders a human pyramid of fifteen bodies, the magician who would turn handkerchiefs into little chickens (not to forget the eggs), and the blond lady dwarf, strong and supple, who looked like a child and sang with her sweet and measured voice old nursery songs, while

52

balanced on the head of a monkey.

The circus had just come (so said its poster) from "a triumphant tour of China, Africa, Japan, Oslo and Rio de Janeiro", and Vercingetorix thought the animals looked somewhat tired, the garlands of lights were missing their bulbs, the tent was worn. The grey and windy morning of their arrival did not seem propitious. Two men in costume—one a Chinese, the other a preacher—were going up and down the main street, throwing paper streamers from side to side and blowing a loud trumpet.

Vercingetorix could not attend the opening or any of the other performances because the next day he disappeared, brutally pushed into the back of a car without license plates, whose type was well-known and feared throughout the town. He thought of the blue canary which might die of hunger and of the blond lady dwarf, strong and supple, who looked like a child and sang with her sweet and measured voice old nursery songs, while dancing on the monkey's head.

He had seen her the previous evening, perched at a table in a bar near the circus, complaining that her tea was not hot and that her piece of cake tasted sour. Her short delicate legs sheathed in knitted white stockings kicked furiously against the table. The waiter, amused by her fit of anger, removed neither tea nor cake, provoking the little lady even further. She had pinned a silver star in her blond hair and her cheeks were highlighted by rouge and by fury. She was wearing a white crêpe dress, like a doll's, and pink dancing slippers which were terribly small. Vercinterorix wondered how a woman of such tiny dimensions could give vent to so much rage; he was also intrigued by the fact that her portion of cake topped with cream and strawberries was larger than her

53

foot. It annoyed him that the waiter should laugh at her and ignore her complaints. He intervened, but unsuccessfully, as she turned toward him and said sharply, "This is my business. I'm perfectly capable of looking after myself."

After which she hit the table with knife and fork—they looked so big in her tiny hands—spat upon the ground and defiantly spilled her drink. This froze the laughter on the waiter's lips. As he went to wipe the table, taking advantage of his proximity, she scratched his face with her fingers, childlike, but with nails as sharp as claws.

As the car sped through the streets, the few pedestrians went running to hide under archways or behind corners; soon the town was empty as under a nuclear alarm. Vercingetorix thought once again of the lady dwarf and of the circus which he would not see.

The next two years(if there was still any point in measuring time by the clock, when it seemed like ten years to him and twenty to his friend suffering agonies about him) Vercingetorix spent in a camp for the disappeared. It was a remote place, far from the town, set between a stony mountain and a cement factory which covered with dust the barracks and the trees in the vicinity. It was a ghost village, tinted greenish-yellow by the cement, with no road or path leading to it. The pipelines, the platforms, the rotating mixers and the chimneys standing in the midst of that loneliness looked like dusty and arthritic robots, all movement lost—a heap of rusty scrap-iron left over from a civilization after apocalypse.

Vercingetorix did not know whether the cement factory had existed before his arrival or had been built for the first group of disappeared. If it existed before, it had probably stopped working and had been put back into action for their use. Nobody knew of this cement factory whose grit covered people's eyes and clothes, turned the trees into ashen sticks, the mountains into heaps of cardboard. Nobody knew of the disappeared either, trapped in the sands of oblivion and death, like a column of ants working their tunnels while the distant city slept.

This was a place of passage. The disappeared remained at the cement factory for a few weeks, a couple of months at most. Vercingetorix knew they would be moved again soon, and no doubt this move would be their last. He wouldn't be returned home (to the blue canary and the blond dwarf of the circus), he would be thrown from a plane to the bottom of the sea ("Valéry had not thought of this kind of *cimetière marin*," mused Ecks later) or would end up in a mass grave improvised in some suburban plot. Yet death started here, in this wave of cement powder which covered them as if they already were corpses or funereal statues; it was useless to try to remove it from their eyes or mouth: it coloured them all alike with a greenish yellow tint until they looked like ghosts, spitting blood and dust, vomiting bile and dust, their bones, turned to dust, breaking under the blows.

Vercingetorix could not believe that, while they were turning into greenish skeletons at the foot of the mountain, elsewhere life continued as before. "We have disappeared, yet out there the circus opens, the acrobatic twins perform their somersaults, tigers leap through hoops of fire and the lady dwarf dances on the monkey's head. Children will go to school, women will give birth and the newspapers will examine in detail the latest goal of the nation's top player, the centre forward so often described as 'the wizard of football'; and the world will not know of the existence of this phantasma, its rachitic, grey trees, its population disintegrating from coughs, haemorrhages, electrodes and paralysis.''

At times, while performing the tasks assigned to him, Vercingetorix was aware of his strong body and still-agile muscles, in spite of the dust penetrating the skin and attacking the tissues. And this awareness would bring him a clear image of two distinct worlds, parallel yet unknown to each other, remote and independent, like two spheres rotating for ever in the silent blue of space. No doubt, people were going to the cinema at this very moment when he was lifting a heavy stone from one place to another, under the watchful eye of a soldier who a moment later would order him—blind with cement dust, his eyelashes yellow, his lips dry and cracking—to return it to its former place.[1] Others were going to work, women prepared meals or read, clocks were striking in offices while secretaries took notes. Yet, men and women disappeared from the city, leaving empty houses, the dog chewing a lonely bone, and the lit stove heating the milk for breakfast. And here the cement was suffocating, weakening, driving them mad.

Like something out of Breughel, Ecks observed. The city, like an immense tower of many storeys, each independent from the other, each operating without the slightest suspicion of the others' existence; each storey with its timetable, routine, laws, codes, functioning in parallel to the others, yet secret and incommunicable. On the lower floors torture, rape and death took place; on the upper ones, films, football games and school lessons. Vercingetorix thought that in order not to go mad it was better to shut out the different levels of the tower, forget any common language, and accept Babel.

Vercingetorix survived, thanks to his talent as a cook (much appreciated by the guards), and also thanks to his strong lungs which, like steel mesh, filtered the scum for two years.

When he was finally freed together with a few other wretches, Vercingetorix was the same age as Jesus at the time of His crucifixion. Yet he looked much older, conditions in the camp not being particularly good for the complexion.

The first thing he did when they let him out was to go to the vacant lot where the circus had had its tent. He wanted to see the lady dwarf with the silver star in her hair. Many things had changed during his absence. The circus was touring the United States and would not be coming that year. Vercingetorix sent them a postcard addressed to some big city where he supposed they might be performing.

But he was tired of things that appeared and disappeared without warning, and he no longer felt comfortable in the city. At night he remembered the cement factory and how he had lived in that ghostly place, banished from all the world, where truckloads of prisoners came or went covered in greenish dust. Perhaps at this very moment, as he lay smoking stretched on his bed and thinking of a factory killing them bit by bit, somewhere, not far from his narrow bed and his green canary (the blue one had died of course), there would be another camp, another hell, with its inmates dying without trace, either thrown into the sea or buried in common graves, no name, no memory. And he couldn't live with this thought.

One day he heard the circus had arrived in Bahía Blanca, where he had once been as a child, accompanying his father on a business trip. He thought that this was a good opportunity to leave. He was sure that if he remained, he would be taken again on some pretext or other, to fill once again his lungs with iron or cement; or if they didn't take him, it would be someone else. In the meantime people would carry on as normal, on the surface at least, eating in restaurants, going to the cinema or to school, celebrating birthdays, christening the newborns, and the generals, solemn and anachronistic as wind-up dolls, delivering their speeches by the light of arc lamps and national flags.

1. Vercingtorix noticed that the soldiers and officers were predisposed not only to violence but to poetry. Often the prisoners were ordered to gather in the yard and the commander, his voice trembling, his eyes sparkling with emotion, would read them his verses, penned in the solitude of the dusty camp—hymns to love of country, the beauty of the flag, the honour of the Armed Forces, their bloody battle against The Enemy, the sun, the military calling, strong family values and the Church. Applause was obligatory and there were penalties for those whose applause was judged deficient in sincerity.

Another novelty was the commandant's requirement that prisoners with university degrees (and there were many) should come forward and give an exalted appreciation of the text which had just been read. Often the poet himself and his lower officers were so moved by the analysis and presentation of the beauty of his poems that they burst into tears. Official interest grew to such an extent that the Army established a small press dedicated to bringing out the work of its valiant guardians of the law. Since the books didn't sell, the newspapers were obliged to carry selections of military poetry in their Sunday supplements, with the result that their sales dropped considerably.

Sometimes, Vercingetorix remembered, there were even *cantatas* involving the prisoners as a chorus. Thus they all had to learn by heart the poem of Lieutenant Miguel Echanis, a camp instructor, which went:

"What are you?"

"Prisoners" (answered the chorus).

"What do prisoners do?"

"Obey."

"Who are we?"

"Soldiers."

"What do soldiers do?"

"Kill."

"Whom do we kill?"

"Enemies of the Fatherland."

The task of appraising this text fell first upon Professor Julio Castro (whose white and venerable head was full of lice). He stressed the symmetry of the lines, while another prisoner, a musician, expanded further that such symmetry fell quite within the tradition of parallelism stretching back to the Bible. A teacher highlighted the lyrical impulse of the piece (perhaps showing the influence of germanic sagas—so said a blond philosophy student). After this it became customary to perform the work once every day.

At the camp entrance stood a sign which said in large letters: A HEALTHY BODY IN A HEALTHY MIND. The dust from the factory settled on the thin trees, the wooden platform to which prisoners were tied, the

59

mountainside and the letters of the sign. One of the disappeared was put in charge of keeping it clean. The dust fell so fast that no sooner had she finished the last letter, than she had to start again on the first.

The Journey, X: Life in the Cities

Ecks is sitting on a bench by the square, facing the cathedral. Vercingetorix is standing, contemplating the facade, a bit overdone for his taste. They have nothing else to do, being relatively young, foreign (yet not tourists) and without money. Ecks grabs a page of newspaper flying in the wind and begins to read, while smoking. Not far from him children play, coaches unload crowds of tourists, street vendors sell lemonades, postcards and toffee apples.

Vercingetorix is so tall and brawny that his clothes always give the impression of being a little short and too tight on him, like those of a scarecrow. The morning is warm and he is happy to watch the children playing in the square, especially the little girls for whom he feels a helpless attraction. His red hair sticking up on the top of his head, white socks showing beneath trousers which hardly reach his ankles, he is perhaps waiting for a puff of wind to steer either hoop or balloon in his direction, giving him the opportunity to start a conversation. Since he left home, this time disappearing by his own means, all he wants is to converse, be it with little girls or dwarf ladies.

Ecks is more inclined to talk to elderly people, of either sex, inquiring with sincere concern about their health, pensions and grandchildren.

Suddenly a child dressed in white runs backwards without looking and trips against the robust legs of Vercingetorix; at first she only sees the grey material of his trousers, worn but clean, then slowly shifting her eyes from his legs, she gazes up at him:

"Hello!" says Vercingetorix, smiling.

She looks back thoughtfully and he becomes aware of her meticulous and merciless stare—taking in the freckles on his forehead, the bluish smallpox scars, the wiry red moustache, the hairs in his nostrils and the blue slits of his eyes. He trembles under that rigorous stare, but knows that it is necessary: neither a child nor a cat give their confidence without this sort of examination.

Ecks leans his head against the back of the bench, wanting to close his eyes and let the warm sunlight lull him to sleep.

"Will she approve of me?" Vercingetorix asks himself with concern. Why does he always feel so vulnerable in the presence of children?

On the point of falling asleep, Ecks is shaken upright by a municipal guard in uniform who waves a ticket in front of him. He slowly opens his eyes (nothing he hates more than being awoken on the point of dozing off) and looks up in surprise. Birds are hiding in the branches; a rat is scuttling across the square towards a hole in the drain; children squeal. Without understanding, Ecks stares at that scrap of paper in the guard's hand.

"Hello," comes the girl's reply, and Vercingetorix senses with relief that he has passed the test. Then the child touches his knee, as if so tall a man might not be entirely real, might be on stilts or something.

"It is all me!" explains Vercingetorix, who has

understood her suspicion.

Standing dauntless before Ecks, the municipal guard continues holding out the ticket. Since Ecks does not understand, the guard explains that he must pay for sitting on a public bench in front of the cathedral. Ecks becomes angry.

Crouching down, Vercingetorix is tying the little girl's shoe-laces. Pigeons are fluttering around her because she's eating a slice of bread and there are crumbs on the ground. Ecks refuses to pay; he is a foreigner, does not know the laws of this country and has the right to question them. Vercingetorix has gone to buy the child a bag of peanuts and is now telling her a long tale of boats drifting out to sea.

The municipal guard is so enraged by Eck's refusal to pay or leave the bench, that he is now trying to push him off. Attracted by the din they are making, Vercingetorix approaches, holding the child by the hand. Other people are surrounding Ecks, making comments in the vein of "Would you believe it?" or "What have we come to?" or "Things are not what they used to be". Obviously they are on the side of the municipal guard, who is merely performing his duty, against Ecks, who not only is a foreigner, but also assumes he has the right to use public property without paying. Vercingetorix advances, elbowing his way, (he has had to leave the little girl by a water fountain promising to be back straightaway) and rescues Ecks from the crowd, just as he is about to deliver a sermon on freedom, human rights and the meaning of authority, and all in that mixture of languages which comes to him whenever he is angry.

"Let's go," Vercingetorix orders in their native tongue, dragging him by the arm.

"I just wanted to teach them about freedom," explains Ecks as he is almost lifted into the air by his friend.

An old white-haired woman is following them. As Vercingetorix looks around the fountain to find, sadly, that the little girl has gone, the woman catches up with them. Looking closely at Ecks and smiling mischievously she says, "I think that water, light, films and buses should also be free."

In the centre of the tapestry stands the Creator of the Universe, making the sign of the benediction with one hand and holding an open book in the other; behind him are inscribed the words Rex Fortis *and in a circle around him,* Dixit Quoque Deus Fiat Lux Et Facta Est Lux *(Then God said: Let there be Light and there was Light).*

The Journey, XI: The Habits of Ecks

There are times when Ecks reads on the bus simply to provoke his fellow passengers. He chooses a large book and a crowded bus. Once assured of standing room, he leans his book against the shoulders of the passenger in front as on a lectern, and turns the pages digging his elbow in the sternum of the man on his left, whose sad bovine look takes on a certain sparkle whenever one of his ribs is threatened. Normally this gives rise to animated discussions around Ecks (who refuses to close his book), between those who would care to go on reading over his shoulder and the others who would rather throw the volume out of the window. This assumes that there is an open window in the bus, for, as Ecks has frequently observed, living in crowded conditions seems to go hand in hand with poor ventilation.

Ecks describes this system of enforced reading as his literacy campaign, though he admits his methods are not orthodox. During periods of greatest public deprivation (for example when some novelized soap opera is all the rage, or when the government of the day imposes its censorship on the more challenging books), Ecks feel no scruples in using even pornography, which can be depended upon to awaken the interest of schoolboys, married men and those women who read little because they travel little. Taking advantage of the interest aroused, Ecks goes on to recommend other equally pornographic works by J.D. Salinger, Foucault, Cortázar.

Whenever these overt activities are put a stop to, he carries in his pocket, by way of a secret line of attack, a list of carefully selected books which he can slip into the hands of the passenger enjoying a quick side-glance at page 51 of his *Tristram Shandy*.

Once, travelling on the long stretch between the City cemetery and the harbour with Nabakov's *Ada* (or is it *Ardour*?) open in front of him, Ecks noticed that the elderly lady by his side was engrossed in his book. As he turned the pages slowly, suspecting that her eyesight was none too good, she whispered into his ear as if confiding a secret to a friend: "When I was young, I too was an anarchist."

To which Ecks cryptically replied, "Pleasure is desire."

FROM THE DAILIES

A young woman, who had arrived in New York only five days previously from a small town in the Mid-West, without either friends or relatives in the city, was seen walking about in the streets during an eight-hour period carrying a sign with the following message:

"I'm very lonely. Please someone talk to me."

Cars passed, pedestrians hurried by, puffs of hot steam rose from the grids ventilating the Subway, shop windows glittered as night fell. Kate's feet hurt from so much walking in a city which has the highest ratio of neurotics in the world.

Ecks went to the doctor because he felt depressed.

"What's your problem?" the doctor asked (he was one of those low-priced ones who can afford only four-and-a-half minutes for each patient, but who assume that every patient can be treated with one of three or four prescriptions). "I'm depressed," Ecks muttered softly in reply. The doctor looked surprised. Two minutes gone by. "Call that a problem? We're all depressed."

A whiff of ketchup and fries wafts from the fast-food places; plastic greenery spills from window boxes. Huge movie hoardings. Red and green neon. People go rushing by, curiously looking—or not looking—at the sign saying, "I'm very lonely. Please someone talk to me." Intimidating suggestion.

Cars stop for the traffic lights, engines purring; their glittering headlamps and shrill horns nosing ahead, they are poised for the signal like race horses waiting for the starting pistol. And they're off! The pedestrians, well-schooled in the norms of crossing, now must wait their turn inside the white lines, restless, like horses at the gate.

"Try a double whiskey at night and relax," advises the doctor.

"But I feel something strange here." On this side of the stomach, like a small animal, trapped, protesting.

"So what am I supposed to do about it?" the doctor checks his watch. Four minutes.

At night the lights convey some agony, despite their glitter and colours. Darkness fills the bottoms of gardens and backs of houses. Strains of music eddy from the bars, syncopated by the thumps of the pinball machines. The platinum ball shoots out, hits a target, a red bulb lights up, now aim for the red king of hearts and knock him down. Pinball beats whiskey, muses Eck; too bad only losers play.

68

Kate wanders on. Long lines of cars wait to fill up at the service stations; empty beercans roll—"Leave your litter here"—but the ball, shot with excessive vigour, passes the red king of hearts without touching and pathetically ends up in a hole in the centre from which the flippers cannot rescue it: another game lost.

The papers report that Kate killed herself around midnight on a bench in the square—an overdose of barbituates. Ecks calms down the restless animal in his stomach with a double whiskey: "Get drunk, you bastard."

Outside the circle which surrounds the Creator of the Universe a larger circle is drawn occupying the central portion of the tapestry (of whose original six metres only three metres and sixty-five centimetres remain). This larger circle is divided into eight sections, of varying sizes, which represent different moments of the creation. In the first, directly over the head of the Creator, a dove, symbol of the spirit of God, is poised above the waters. The script says: Spiritus Dei ferebatur super aquas *(The Spirit of God moved upon the face of the waters).*

The haloed dove displays wonderfully elaborated wings and the waters over which it flies are green.

Within the circle surrounding the Creator (Let there be Light) in the segment to the left of the dove poised above the waters, stands an angel with wings, long garments and hand on his breast. The angel floats over a field with reeds and flowering canes.

Did the anonymous weaver of the tapestry—if indeed there was only one-—know that canes flower but once every hundred years, so that it is unlikely that this would happen twice during a single lifetime?

The angel in this segment of the tapestry is the angel of darkness and holds a torch in his left hand. On the ochre background of the weave (discoloured by time) is written: Tenebrae erant super faciem abissi *(Darkness was upon the face of the deep).*

The Journey, XII: The Fallen Angel

Whenever Ecks gets drunk—which doesn't happen often because alcohol upsets his liver—he has the most wonderful adventures. Drinking makes him romantic: floating like a dove over the waters, he conceives tender passions for unknown beings whom he follows from afar, as sailors follow the flight of distant birds with their binoculars.

During his travels Ecks came to an island in M., tropical in its vegetation. Its roads were cobbled, large seashells hung from the rooftops covered with branches, amongst which the grass sprouted; steep cliffs descended towards a crystal sea at the bottom of which stones and pebbles glistened.

At first the air, perfumed with camelias and fruit trees—medlars, apricots, lemons, oranges and peaches—affected Ecks. Fresh from the asphalt of the cities, he experienced a loss of vitality, similar to that post-coital state which Ovid cynically described as *melancholia*.

The place on the island where Ecks came had a mystical name: Pueblo de Dios. Years before (not knowing that one day in his aimless wanderings he would end up there, like the traveller who sets out for a precise destination but is thrown by a storm onto the shores of an unknown land) Ecks had read that during the Middle Ages this village gave shelter and home to a saintly man.

Here, after a dissolute youth at court, he had dedicated himself to writing books in many languages to the honour of God, and had also studied the local flora. He learned to distill liquor—a practice which brought him both closer to God and nearer to cirrhosis of the liver, for the properties of this drink he naively confused with those of the philosopher's stone.

The story goes that as a knight at court, beloved of kings and favoured by the ladies, he had for some time assailed a young woman with the most ingenious and worldly persuasions. One morning he pursued her on horseback to the cloisters of a church famed for its alabaster tombs. The woman entered, without so much as casting a look on him. The knight followed, determined to have speech with her. Suddenly she turned and uncovered her chest, disfigured by cancer. Moved by this revelation, the young knight abandoned his worldly ways, gave up all forms of hunting in which he so excelled, and dedicated himself to study, to the love of God, and to distilling brandy in his free time.

Ecks rested for a while on one of the terraces of the village shaded by a vine whose grapes, though unripe, still filled the air with fragrance. Beer and refreshments were served on wicker tables. From the pergola hung sea shells harvested in times when heavy traffic and pollution had not yet begun to destroy the oceans. Empty bottles filtered the brilliant light of the sun. A monstrous green parrot was gibbering in its cage, mixing words from different languages, something familiar to Ecks whose own conversation also frequently combined sounds of various tongues. Dogs came and went among the tables. A young and lively one approached him with demonstrations of affection. Ecks felt grateful: he had visited many cities and countries without receiving a single greeting or even the acknowledgement of a smile.

Dizzy with scents and the memory of Ramón Llull, that holy man and distiller of brandy who praised God in various idioms, Ecks sat under the unripe grapes—the puppy by his side—and looked with contentment at the plants growing out of crevices in the rough wall before him. He ordered a double brandy in homage to the mystic who, besides his apostolic work, had written an *Ars Navigandi* and a study of tides, *Why does the English Channel Flow Backwards and Forwards?*, in which he neatly upheld that the world was round. Ecks breathed deeply, caressed by the sunlight. Many tourists, lightly clothed as warranted by the climate, had joined him on the terrace. Ecks noticed an older woman sitting alone, discreetly sipping tea. Full of the ripe smell of fallen apricots, of the murmur of a stream which flowed not far off through mosses and blackberries, and affected most of all by the double brandy, Ecks gave her the benediction of an enraptured smile which filled the air with promise.

She was plump and fair, with a white complexion, thin lips and small blue eyes encircled by long and silky eyelashes. Time had accumulated layers of fat around her body which gave her that compact and rotund appearance, and Ecks imagined the heat, the extraordinary whiteness and palpable softness of that slowly melting flesh, and he loved her.

He was fascinated by her face of an aging cherub, fattened by the joys of heaven. The question of the sex of angels (he was quite sure that there were both boy-angels with small penises and undeveloped testicles and girl-angels with their clefts delicately lined and only slightly darker than the rest of their bodies) occupied

Ecks, but the problem of their age concerned him more. For some perverse reason, during the course of centuries painters and theologians have assumed that only male adolescents could achieve angelic stature. Ecks instead believed that only fallen angels were adolescents—like fallen, unripe apricots—whereas the good angels were older, even doddery, their members dangling flaccid with age, their heads occasionally bald, males and females alike.

Ecks admired this lady's immaculate complexion, her plump cheeks beginning to droop, those fine lips almost lost among the grooves of flesh at the corners of her mouth, her thick and delicately silvered hair and the white, smooth hands sweetly holding her cup of tea. She was alone, sitting with her back to the wall of rough stones in whose crevices plants were sprouting. She smiled benevolently whenever the half-naked children ran in excited bursts out of the sunshine, knocking over the chairs by her side. Her fingers twined around the handle of the cup, her head tilted, she took in the air, the fragrance of the trees, and smiled with pleasure for being there. The plain green dress which allowed her fat white arms to roll out of its short sleeves bewitched Ecks. Faced with the serenity and calm of her countenance, he realized he was in the presence of one of those mature angels ignored by painters and theologians. By the third brandy Ecks (who never carried his drink very well) clearly remembered—unlike most exiles unable to recall anything but the odd folkloric and detestable song—verses from the poets of the *dolce stil novo*:

> *You, who do breach mine eyes and touch the heart*
> *And start the mind from her brief reveries,*
> *Might pluck my life and agony apart.*

Saw you how love assaileth her with sighs...

He also remembered those streets where Dante had wandered before *his* exile, as much in love with Beatrice as with his fellow-poet Guido Guinizelli.

Just as Ecks was about to recite to the lady these lines of Cavalcanti, she turned towards him inquiring in faulty Spanish (which he found adorable) about the times of trains. Ecks hastened to find out and returned with some flowers he had picked on the spot. He asked permission to sit with her at her table. She assented with a smile. Ecks judged that she was at least thirty-five years older than himself, which meant that when he was fifteen (yes, he *was* fifteen once) she had already turned fifty. Now she would be nearer sixty-eight. Graciously she accepted his flowers, smiling without looking at anyone in particular. "It is because she is an angel," thought Ecks, "and angels do not need any pretext to smile, such is their condition. Her smile partakes of grace and expresses the harmony and order of the universe."

The dog had followed him and was now lying in front of them, fatigued with the heat. "That's good, he is not jealous," thought Ecks. "Neither is she." As the woman spoke in a language Ecks did not understand, making conversation was rather tricky; all the same, instead of being depressed by this as he might normally have been, Ecks found it stimulating and broke into an uninhibited monologue.

"Ecks is my name," he told her. "For the past few years, due to special circumstances having more to do with the way the world turns than with my personal wishes, I have travelled from one place to another without any firm direction. You are a most beautiful woman," he added, aware that he was using the terms

76

of an old-fashioned seducer, eminently suitable on the present occasion. "Very old/very modern" he quoted to himself (was it Ruben Darío or Victor Hugo?).

It is probable that she did not understand what he said, nor did she inform him of her name, age, religion, political affiliations, country of origin, etc. But these declarations which might interest an immigration officer did not interest Ecks. He was convinced that she was Swedish, five times a grandmother, that she had been widowed for several years (thus eliminating any possible or unwelcome competition), and was holidaying alone.

Ecks noticed that despite the plumpness of her upper arms, her wrists were almost slender. Her elbows, instead of ending in a point like lemons as they normally do, were so cushioned with flesh that they disappeared into the intimacy of a cavity covered with little crevices and wrinkles.

Whether or not she managed to understand Ecks (who was by now digressing into a lengthy recital of cities, women and wars), the woman unexpectedly introduced new subjects, making comments which enchanted Ecks. "I have sent my dog to a school," he thought he heard her say, "to learn English, because he only understands Swedish: he is making good progress and now responds correctly to commands like *Sit down*." Ecks found this intriguing; he then asked her whether the dog might stand up if one gave him the same command in Spanish. She did not understand his question.

The woman was holding a straw basket with a large dahlia embroidered on the side. Ecks felt he loved the basket and the dahlia as well, just as he loved the gold bracelets around her chubby white arms, the wicker chairs on the terrace, the feet of the other tourists, and even the sweat of the proprietor, who did not bathe often, as happens among Europeans. But when he glanced under the table and saw that the woman was wearing sandals, more than anything else (more than the young girl with wet hair hanging down which tasted of seawater and marigolds, and who eyed him with curiosity while obscenely eating an apricot which she bit cruelly with sadistic lips) Ecks loved those pink sandals. Had he been a sex maniac (which, like everybody else, he was in his fantasies) Ecks would have been a dedicated pursuer of women in sandals. Whether partly covering the foot (thus revealing tantalizing bits of flesh) or standing daintily in a shop window or reclined on a carpet, sandals always provoked intense excitement in Ecks. The elegant models—the classic cross-strap with a slender heel— produced emotions which verged on lyricism. He could look at them at length, isolating them from the feet on which they rested, and study them as detached objects, allowing his imagination to soar. On the other hand flatties, with soles as thin as shaving blades and a single strap tied around the ankle, provoked frankly erotic sensations. In this case the sandals were of the palest rose, in considerable harmony with the person of the wearer. They left parts of her chubby feet uncovered, the bouncy little pads of her naked toes contrasting with the narrow white ankles.

Looking respectfully at the water-blue eyes of the noble lady, Ecks (drunk with sunshine and with the brandy distilled between bouts of theology and science) spoke of many things, while she contentedly drank her tea with movements both skilled and delicate. She did not need to understand, nor did Ecks need to be listened to—a convention upon which depends the success of most couples in the world.

When she had finished her drink and made to stand up (moving the chair away from the table for her ample body to shift less awkwardly between the two), Ecks without hesitation stood as well. (He was in the middle of a diatribe on the World Bank's plan to solve the problem of absolute poverty among six hundred million people, whereby Mr MacNamara invited the poor to reproduce less, given their irresponsible tendency towards mating.) The dog, obligingly, stood up also.

After they left the terrace and its vine pergola, they took the cobbled road, wherever this might lead, Ecks happily offering a chivalrous arm to the lady and she leaning on it. He looked back, dazed with sunlight and alcohol, at the mocking, indifferent smile of the young girl with wet hair and breasts stuck against her T-shirt, now biting into a peach, as if it were something else. It was very hot; above the sound of crickets and cicadas, he thought he heard the croaking of frogs. The road climbed steeply towards the blue mountain whose slopes were covered in thick vegetation.

The two walked through the streets of the little town, a kindly son supporting his elderly mother, an orphan who had found a mother's love. Both were talking in their own language, but from time to time the lady signalled to Ecks to admire the broad twisted trunk of a carob or an ancient olive tree, or pointed out a falcon hovering above the mountain top, her blue eyes raised to follow its flight. In his turn, Ecks pointed out the purple exhuberance of the bougainvilleas, discovered a torrent flowing between rocks and bushes. They passed the washing place under its roof covered with ivy, crossed the bridge made of tree trunks over a dry riverbed, and came to the square with its arbour of flowers under whose wedding arch they walked to the entrance of her hotel.

There were pots in the window of her room with geraniums, ferns and mimosas. The green blinds filtered the sunlight; bells of grazing sheep rang in the distance. On the table in the small sitting area stood two glasses and a plant with long, slim leaves traversed by a net of fine yellow veins; not knowing its name, Ecks baptized it without hesitation, "Tiger's tail". He sat in one of the two wicker chairs; beyond, he could see the bedroom, a large ancient bed with a carved wooden back and a stocky four-door wardrobe.

The lady went to the wardrobe and brought out a thermos from which she poured Ecks a glass of cold tea. Ecks accepted with pleasure. He liked the serene atmosphere of the room, the blessing which her presence transmitted to all things, and liked the white outline of the brassiere beneath her dress, from which spilled her enormous breasts.

The courtship was slow and difficult, yet not devoid of those delicate and intimate gestures which always delighted Ecks. At first she resisted, giving lengthy and well-reasoned explanations in a language he did not understand but whose sounds pleased him. When she finished speaking—they were still sitting in the small sitting room with their glasses of tea—Ecks hooked his thumb around hers. Her thumb—how he enjoyed the plumpness of that flesh which swelled out, then thinned towards the tip—how immaculately white it was. An innocent, fat, seraphic thumb that had never known human touch. She was ticklish; she began coquettishly to laugh, and he laughed with her. The timidity of this noble lady must be overcome or he would be affected by it. Thus Ecks launched into a long speech, this time on tapestries. Though he had no idea why he should tell her about the Crakow weavings, saved from the Nazis by the daring action of Polish patriots, he spoke with such passion on the subject that there seemed to be nothing else worth talking about. He described the small swift boats, their secret journeys by which finally the tapestries came safely to Canada, and spoke of the risks run and accidents suffered. With growing enthusiasm, touched perhaps by the tone of his voice or what little she could make out of his story, the lady began to look into his eyes. Her gaze was celestial, of young leaves and fresh water, demure yet exciting. Ecks knew that he had succeeded in overcoming her modesty.

He asked to be allowed to look at her while she undressed. At first she misunderstood and, turning away from him, resisted his attempts to help her. But Ecks begged her with such tender eyes that she finally turned to him. He undid the narrow leather belt which, buried in the flesh of her waist, held the dress in place; gently removed it and hung it, symbol of her chastity, over the windowsill. He then held her in his arms to undo the long zip at the back of the dress; he was amazed to discover that his arms could not reach round her. It did not matter: he loved her all the more. He embraced her for a few moments, softly buried in that marvellous mountain of flesh, white smooth flesh, in which the veins were drawn like thin blue rivers.

Trembling and unsure, she let him continue, glancing at him from time to time with surprise.

The zip was undone, but Ecks wanted her to leave

the dress on until he had removed her underwear, so that he could see her majestic body naked all at once. Holding her against him by the waist, he bent down and put his hand under the dress. Caressing fabulous masses which parted warmly beneath his fingers, he advanced through clouds of cotton which, touched, revealed wells of darkness, deep as craters of the moon. There started the edge of her underpants; as he had imagined, they were wide long silken ones, probably white or rose, with narrow vertical stripes of the same colour, which he could feel in the thin cloth. Excited, he let his hand slip down to where her fat thighs came together in a thin straight line. From this angle her feet looked as white, puffy and childlike as those of a angel by Titian.

The brassiere of strong cotton was easily undone; with satisfaction Ecks heard the click of the fastener opening, and unhooking the straps over the arch of her shoulders, received those tumbling breasts, milk-white and springy, which spilled out of his hands in abundant folds.

Then he made her stand facing him, the better to see her splendid nakedness, those vast legs clinging together, slightly knock-kneed. Her mound of Venus was hairless save for a few pale, almost invisible threads; under her skin the blue veins ran. Her nipples were two tiny violets on a monumental ground. Ecks gazed at her as at a creature from another planet, an imaginary being only to be glimpsed in dreams or fantastical old engravings.

To the right of the Creator of the Universe holding the open book—whereon we perceive five mystic letters drawn, S C S on one side, D and S on the other—this right segment of the tapestry portrays a second angel with slightly taller wings facing the angel to the left of the Creator. An angel in pilgrim's dress walking somewhere. In this section the colours are brighter and more luminous. It is the Angel of Light, as the Latin inscription makes clear.

The Journey, XIII: The Island

The following day Ecks returned to the terrace under the vines. This time he ordered a soft drink. Nothing had changed there: the purple bougainvilleas hung in blazing wreaths down the stony walls. The apricots fell juicily to the ground and the stray dog, infected by the general calm, was dozing in the shade. Feeling drowzy himself, Ecks reclined against the back of the wicker chair, when suddenly a whistle pierced the air and both he and the dog raised their heads. The girl he had seen the previous day was coming, uninhibited and strong, wearing the same dirty, faded T-shirt, swinging her tanned hips, her wet hair glued to the contours of a young face. Once again she looked as if she'd just risen from the sea. The water drops remained tight on her pores like miniature lenses. He thought of those globes with tiny coloured pebbles, plant filaments, splinters of glass and beads, through whose opal surface one imagines mysterious worlds which might lie at the bottom of the sea or those curious planets floating through the heavens.

The girl was bursting with youth; with that radiant beauty which, more than a quality of feature or of line, is the result of organic perfection which only later would begin to fall apart, breaking its essential but precarious harmony. Future years would put out of line all those elements which were now so gracefully balanced. The hips would thicken, the taut, bronzed tissues of her breasts lose their elasticity, early lines would score that polished skin; a vulgar twist would mar the full lips and an obscene sparkle glitter in those dark and provocative eyes. Like the Creator in the tapestry, who orders and watches over his creatures, already knowing their future, divining in the present what shall come to pass, so Ecks watched the girl who advanced towards him with firm steps, beating the ground with her frayed espadrilles. There was defiance as well as provocation in her youth, the awareness of a body in its prime, the certainty that her physical allure—splendid as the sun, the sea, the golden sand of the beaches, or the flight of falcons—deserved pleasure, gratitude, homage. Ecks felt immediately inhibited. Hers was the impunity of the strong and healthy, the vanity and pride of the beautiful. Those legs curving splendidly at the thighs, that skin tone, happy gift of racial mixture which a painter might labour in vain to imitate with his tints, demanded attention. The shirt, carelessly worn, revealed the firmness of her breasts: breasts of baked clay, rounded in perfect symmetry with her hips, each breast fronted by a tempting grape.

You might find one more intelligent...maybe..., thought Ecks, or more sensitive or impressionable, but there could scarcely be a finer physical specimen. When she sat at his table (without asking permission or wondering if she was disturbing him), he felt like neighing. But he was a sophisticated and civilized being, accustomed to control and repress his impulses, unlike this beautiful young mare.

She looked at him mockingly, remembering, no

doubt, the episode of the previous day, when he was half-drunk with brandy and sunshine. Inexplicably, this seemed to give her a certain superiority, an advantage he was not prepared to concede to her insolence. The proprietor—who must have known her—did not come to their table, creating a pause, a brief truce in which Ecks could compose himself, offer her an ice cream as one does to a child (no, no wine), and turn the damned balance of power in his favour.

The girl took out of the pocket of her grey shorts a crumpled pack of cigarettes and offered one to Ecks, who accepted with pleasure, feeling that this gesture established a kind of comradeship between them, the pipe of peace after a war which perhaps had only existed in his male imagination, typically (atypically?) *macho*. The girl's damp hair still shone in the sunlight. She must bathe in fountains, streams and rivers like a nymph, thought Ecks. He thought also how dogs, tired of the heat, will frantically seek out water and lie in it up to the neck—a solitary, ritual ablution—solemnly undergoing the secret restorative contact that exists between a living being and water.

"I don't like being asked who I am and what I do," the girl said, pre-empting a question which Ecks had long ago learned not to ask, such are the uncertainties of modern life.

"The answer would be too complicated. Impossible to state briefly," she continued. "The worst way to start things off. Everybody's a stranger here; if you like you can call me Graciela, given our necessity to refer to people and objects by name. I do wonder how all these different languages came to be. When I first came up against this problem (I was younger then), I felt that the diversity

86

of languages had to be an unnecessary complication; one of those phenomena in life where unnecessary problems arise because nobody has found a simpler way of dealing with them. Simplicity sometimes comes as a result of evolution and not the opposite—it is a synthesis. But now I think differently. The good thing about my age is that one can change ideas often, unlike the old, who may change, but not in those things which they consider important. Paradoxically, they think this is a sign of maturity, though there's no argument to prove that persisting in the same idea or belief has anything to do with maturity. I now think the diversity of languages is a good thing. I don't know why, but I think so. Though sometimes I still wonder what the world would be like if we all spoke alike. So you like old women?''

Ecks had been feeling uncomfortably old since the beginning of the conversation. He stretched himself in his seat, to gain time. He found it difficult to answer Graciela in that concise and direct style of speech she seemed to demand. Often conversation is more a question of style than ideas.

"You see," he answered thoughtfully, "in actual fact I don't have preferences. I mean, I do not find the question of age fundamental. I assume you are referring to the gracious lady who was drinking tea here yesterday morning."

"Yes,"she said without hesitation. "But why do you call her 'gracious lady'? Is she an aristocrat or something? I find the whole business of class distinctions really depressing."

"I'm not referring to that," Ecks tried to defend himself. "It's something else."

"I know a number of men who adore old women.

But they're younger than you. It's like a childhood illness, chicken-pox or something. Even some friends of mine. Frankly I find them rather stupid.''

"I'm not referring to *that* either,'' answered Ecks laconically.

"I think,'' said the girl, "that you'd find it difficult to live without these pronouns of yours. I've just finished a grammar course and I've picked up a lot of usage. Anyway, I'm not interested in the question of the old girl, whether she's an English aristocrat or retired from the chorus line. We get a lot of them here. Actresses of fifth or sixth rank, who once played a bit part in some film produced by Metro or Fox, and now go around like exiled princesses. The kids here take no notice of them, because they're hysterical and bitter. Besides, they're a disaster in bed. Just like the bosses; they don't want efficiency, but slavery. You ever sunbathe?''

"You see,'' answered Ecks, "my skin is rather sensitive. Also, no offense meant because you are not like this, but the spectacle of pale flesh roasting on the beach, while orange peels, empty mineral water bottles and oil stains float on the sea...''

"What do you mean, 'I am not like this'?'' she sternly interrupted.

"Well, you came before pollution, before tankers collided on the high seas, before plastic, before bone defects, motor boats and fuel slicks. Before suntan lotions, rejuvenating creams and marihuana behind the changing rooms. If you allow me to say so, you are like an idea free from historical circumstances.''

She observed him pensively

"If I understand you correctly, you say this in spite of the fact that I smoke dope, adore the sun and the cinema. Perhaps that old woman was also 'an idea free from historical circumstances', in spite of the fact that her house in Stockholm or London may be full of gadgets, that she makes her yoghurt with an ultrasonic yoghurt-maker, keeps plastic plants, a dishwasher and a video.''.

She looked straight at him and asked, ''Would you do it with me too?''

Ecks started. It was like the time his mother had suddenly opened the door and surprised him engrossed in the innocent task of classifying stamps. Then as now he had the impression of partly deceiving somebody.

''You see...,'' he hesitated, wondering confusedly what she would consider an adequate script for this scene.

''Where would you be without your little pet phrases,'' she interrupted ironically, taking advantage of his hesitation.

''I think I would,'' he said simply.

''So,'' she went on as if his answer confirmed her expectations. ''This,'' she was trying to remember his exact words, ''this 'idea deprived...'—sorry, 'free from historical circumstances' might also be an idea free of objective reality: a reflection of your mind. I can only reason it out so far. The question of reflections seems terribly complicated. I think I shall fail my philosophy exam. Will you ever know (she asked) if what you come to think, or imagine, has anything to do with me or the old woman (and by God she was old), or are we merely the image of your fantasy, of your desire? Our desires are fantasies and it is possible they do not originate from the objects or beings who stimulate us, but from our own minds... Beyond this point I get lost. I feel unwell as when I've eaten too many grapes or slept too long. I don't believe all this thinking is doing my head much good. It's been accustomed to obey for too long, having been the head of a child, and now a woman."

"Two conditions difficult to overcome," declared Ecks with solemnity. "Age frees you from the first, but the second demands a long struggle."

"I don't like parrotting the master's voice," protested Graciela. "I shall fail my philosophy exam. Anyway, what I think I've worked out all on my own," she added darkly. "Nobody prepared me for this. Do you carry condoms?"

Ecks was caught unawares again. "No," he said.

"I guessed as much," she sighed. "Are you the type that expects girls to wreck their health with the pill or aborting in some women-only clinic, or maybe you only choose lovers on the far side of the menopause?"

She sounded annoyed, and Ecks felt guilty. Free from historical circumstances, perhaps, but guilty all the same, as if he had beaten a child.

"I shan't be long," she said, before he was able to apologize. "I'm going to get my things."

She left quickly, jumping over the hot flagstones, crossing the wave of sunshine which wrapped around her. Ecks watched her weave among the bougainvilleas, over the uneven surface of the road, like an inquisitive lizard, intoxicated with her own wisdom.

When she returned, the dog was pissing on the mimosas, with that philosophical expression so typical of dogs in the act. It stopped, cast a glance at the long stream darkening the leaves, then moved unhesitatingly towards the wheels of a car parked nearby. Here it pissed again; there was just enough for a contemptuous sprinkling of bolts, mudguards and tires, greatly to the delight of Ecks, who saw in it a just condemnation of noisy and uncaring modern technology.

Graciela's luggage consisted of a large guitar case. Though he could live without music, Ecks welcomed the girl's idea. He had a pretty good voice and might easily feel like a little strumming and singing. One must remember the role music plays in the life of the younger generation, he thought, ever the eager student of human behaviour.

"I know a place on the beach," Graciela told him. "It's a cave among the rocks. You have to do a bit of climbing first and wade through the water if the tide is high. Do you suffer from vertigo?" Without waiting for his answer, she went on. "Once I had to spend all night up there because the tide was very high. The stupid boy I was with got upset; he had a cramp and was also scared of what his parents might think. They only allowed him to stay out late for those detestable parties where kids do a lot of petting, smoke grass and fall asleep. They think that to spend a night in the open on the beach is not decent. That's parents for you. Mine are the same. Anyway, it was a wonderful night. We could hear the roar of the sea in the dark and, since we had no more matches, we couldn't tell how close it was. We tried to guess from the sound whether it would invade our cave or not; sometimes it does get flooded. We couldn't see each other, which was a good thing because I couldn't bear looking at his face full of fear. Not because he was a boy; I don't think that boys must be less afraid than girls. If he'd been a girl, I would have found it equally irritating. The cave is quite cold at night, being damp, and as I recall it was windy. Strange how the wind sounds stronger in the dark, isn't it? He must have had an attack of hysteria because I could feel him trembling. I don't understand why he hated me. We had both decided together to go to the cave. We hadn't especially liked each other before, but that day we'd got on well. All the same, after that night he hated me, as if the tide had been my fault. Can you think of a better place?''

This was no more than politeness, for Ecks was well aware that she was determined to go to the cave.

''I'll carry the guitar,'' he offered chivalrously.

''Guitar?'' said Graciela, laughing.

She carelessly placed the case on the table (Ecks grabbed a glass that was about to fall off) and clicked open the metal clasps.

There was no guitar inside, but a series of personal effects: underwear, toothbrush, a cracked mirror, socks, an undershirt, two books, a case of coloured pencils, a comb, matchboxes, an empty film spool, three glass balls, a fountain pen and some newspaper cuttings. There was also—Ecks saw with humiliation—a packet of condoms.

Ecks found this a most discreet way of travelling.

By the cliffs the tide is low; but whenever the wind comes up—like a huge bird that sleeps beneath the branches—the waves grow in strength, flood the debris left behind, and surge over the chalky rocks.

From time to time, beaten by the violence of the sea, whole sections of the cliffs plunge into the water; their stony edges appear in the distance, exposed to the saltpetre and sea air, fragments of rock, raising their twisted or pointed forms, like the heads of a monster. It is not rare that at low tide, while on one side of the cliffs the water gently laps the shore, angry waves break foaming on the other side, as if wanting to invade the beach. This is the side favoured by seagulls and lovers, for it is inaccessible and solitary. You see the birds standing on the cliff tops, like watchers petrified in lava, or crusted in salt. Suddenly a croak cuts the air, like a fire-warning or the creak of wood on shipboard; then they come alive. The moment has come to fish—orbiting in widening gyres over the surface of the water—or to take the ritual flight before mating.

On this side of the shore stands a rock resembling now the head of a lion, now the profile of a proud Persian prince.

Indented in the rugged cliffs whose outline retreats

and juts out unevenly, appear a few caves. The first is only big enough to house the nest of a sparrowhawk or some similar bird. The second, though wider, is not much deeper in size: it stands higher than the other, with tufts of grass at the entrance.

The third is a real cave dug into the top of the cliff whose edges from time to time tumble into the sea. It can hardly be noticed from below, from where it looks more like a small hole, narrow and shallow. But it is a real cave, a dark, deep throat opened in the stone, and of a size to offer shelter for several people.

The story goes that from here, in the eighteenth century, the women of the island defended its freedom. The men, inferior in numbers and arms to their attackers, had already been defeated and were retreating in complete disorder. Their womenfolk, climbing up the cliffs to seek refuge in this cave, gathered the weapons of the dead and wounded. As the invaders disembarked triumphantly on the shore, they were met by a shower of bullets and missiles which seemed to be coming from an entire army strategically hidden in the nooks above. Surprised by the women, the conquerors took fright, returned quickly to their boats and sailed back home.

From ancient times we have recognized the attraction that the moon, that remote silvery magnet, exerts over the waves, which now swell to cover the rugged shapes of rocks and promontories, now, tamed and abated, withdraw to the depths of the ocean. It is then that the creatures which live under the sea reveal their secret, clandestine existence.

In another section of the tapestry, to the left of the Angel of Darkness who holds a torch hiding it from the sight of the world, a circle appears, floating on the surface of the water. Within it is inscribed: Fecit Deus firmamentum in medio aquarum *(God made the firmament in the midst of the waters). This symbolizes the creation of the heavens.*

The Journey, XIV: Pueblo de Dios

In the beginning were words, then came abbreviations. From time to time someone comes to Pueblo de Dios suffering from delusions. These men or women are strangers; their speech is a mixture of different tongues which meet in the making of invocations (we should allow both religious and secular senses of this term, for we are speaking of preachers of sorts). The sound of their utterances is as important as the sense, for indeed the prophet speaks not so much to be understood as to be obeyed. (Which is as much as to say: in the beginning was the metaphor, then came abbreviations.) Consider that one of the oldest words in almost all languages (and this study of the chronology of words is a curious business) is the word *Sun*. It is not difficult to find the reason why. Male or female? According to Borges (about whom Ecks harbours ambiguous feelings), those germanic languages which rise to gender give this word female placing. So too the Guaraní Indians of Paraguay and the ancient Japanese refer to a goddess of the sun.

They are strangers, and almost always young, younger than the age of Dante when he says he lost his way in the dark wood. The deluded ones who come to Pueblo de Dios seem to have sprung up from beyond the far horizon, without origins. They acknowledge no country of provenance, carry no luggage, have no friends. The inhabitants do not come out to meet them and walk by their side, as happened with the Hebrew prophet. These prophets don't much mind; as if the aim of their orations, like the aim of poetry, lay in itself alone.

To retain their prestige, it is essential that their appearances be few. For revelations, like miracles, have to be infrequent in order to command attention. Too frequent miracles would break that delicate balance between reality and fantasy, anxiety and comfort on which their acceptance depends.

According to a map drawn by one of the residents of Pueblo de Dios—a certain Morris who arrived there years ago and never managed to leave—the island, and in particular its little town, constitute one of those places where the spiritual energy of the world is polarized. This is proved by the magnetism of its tides, the large amounts of iron ore buried in the heart of its mountain, the angle of the moon, its hot climate and almost total absence of rain (prophets always avoid northern lands), and by the revelations—five in all—which the ancient courtier, writer, theologian, defender of the faith and brandy distiller claimed to have had on the spot.

Graciela loves maps, especially old ones, so she and Ecks often visit Morris, the eccentric stranger. Ecks is also quite intrigued by his pipe collection, the medieval books in his library, the stamp albums with the effigy of Queen Victoria and the plate number (1858) cryptically inscribed on the spine, which can only be deciphered with the magnifying glass.

"Collectors are passionate beings," such is Graciela's opinion; "much more interesting than bureaucrats."

Her use of words is also passionate. They either

overflow with feelings or cut like a scalpel, now devout, now profane. When she called her father a bureaucrat and his hand flew to her cheek, she was a little surprised, like a child who, without understanding it, inappropriately repeats a phrase which on other occasions has been received with approval. Sometimes they forbid whole books like this, full of seemingly inoffensive words, yet which might awaken old dark resentments secretly stored within every man.

The house of the passionate collector is on the mountain slope; a stone house with few windows (almost exempt from openings—as Morris would say in his elaborate speech), and with a large front garden overgrown by trees, bushes and weeds where it is practically impossible to find one's way. Morris has cleared a path among the branches and he distributes copies of a curious guide (a sign of deepest affection) to a few chosen friends who are requested to keep it secret. "All rights reserved; no sale, exchange or copy permitted" is written in Gothic characters on the one he gave Graciela many years before. He had found her crying by the stream because her pet tortoise had escaped and she would never see it again. Ever since, Graciela goes regularly to his house, much to the scandal of the local people who imagine shocking goings-on, both human and zoological, given Graciela's intense love of horses, snakes, beavers and stags, and the eccentricity of Morris, let alone his solitary habits. Morris rarely leaves his house and when he does, people are distrustful of the strange-sounding words he uses. He explains that his tendency to rhetoric is due to the fact that he learned their language by reading writers and philosophers of the sixteenth century. This puts people off even more, since no one else reads such books, in fact no one has even heard of the authors. Despite this they still manage to live, eat, copulate, buy land and sell houses, set up factories and start new businesses, from which the inhabitants deduce that they can do without that sort of reading.

Graciela got into the habit of visiting Morris, and he became enchanted with her. He showed her all his secret treasures, undertook to educate her—given the lamentable state of public education—and took her in whenever she wanted to run away from her father's house, from that man of whom the least that could be said was that he was a "bureaucrat." Morris loved the child without being too protective, without impinging on her freedom, or wanting her to be like him and fit herself to his personality. His own occupations—the many demanding and meticulous tasks of a collector—prevented the education of Graciela from turning into a duty for either of them; it remained a source of mutual entertainment.

Graciela would arrive at his house with a chicken, some ham, a bottle of wine, a watermelon or a few tomatoes which she had picked on her way to the "secret" path leading to his hermitage. Morris was anxious that the girl should leave before the end of the day, to avoid gossip; but he was absent-minded and on occasions Graciela managed to remain until long after midnight. She would always take back something: an unusual stamp with irregular indentations or an unexpected design; one of those books which are no longer read (definitely the most interesting and the most valuable, as Morris used to say) or perhaps an uncommon butterfly which had been caught in the Amazonian jungle and had come into the hands of Morris after a long exchange of letters. Morris hardly ever went out, but maintained a copious correspondence with the rest of the world, much to the annoyance of his postman, who hated his job and—like all postmen—dreamt of a world in which letters were forbidden. Morris did not display any desire to meet his correspondents—men and women of varying origins and ages—because he thought that the letters we write are better than ourselves, and was quite content with the revelations and the mysteries which the reading of a letter implies. He feared disappointment. The only time that one of his correspondents, a woman, announced she was planning to come to Pueblo de Dios to meet him, he became terribly alarmed. Over the course of three years he had exchanged weekly letters with her, not to mention butterflies, sea-shells, old postcards and telegrams dating back to World War I. He then decided to fall ill with a serious disease, even a contagious one requiring quarantine.

His hidden path protects Morris from unwanted visits, and from the migrants and vagabonds who so abound in "periods of poverty and uncertainty", as Morris describes our present times. Ecks on the other hand maintains that all periods have been periods of poverty and uncertainty for those who have no power: our days are no different from the past, except in the number of tyrants, their systematic methods and the cold logic with which they lead the world to madness.

Morris has a terrestrial globe on his desk, next to his collection of rare carved pipes. On it he marks with black pins the various regions which have fallen prey to tyranny. The free zones are becoming smaller and smaller. From day to day a sad and disillusioned Morris transfixes them with his pins until the only clear areas seem to be the oceans.

"This," says Ecks, "takes no account of the fact that their beaches, riverbeds and remoter shores yield mutilated bodies with some frequency nowadays; bodies which, tortured and thrown into the water, have become entangled like weeds among the reefs and sandbanks. *Cimetières marins*, but so different from those described by Valéry, may he rest in peace."

"One must not speak of these horrors," Morris replies. "In such bad taste, too. Deep-sea fishermen find a girl's ruined body in their nets. And what are they to do with it? For to find a dead person is to become implicated in crime. Those lovely shores where no longer drift mysterious galleys or white-bellied boats in the shallows, but corpses with disfigured faces. Tell me, what is the coast with the greatest number of these cemeteries? Perhaps I'd better mark-off all these seas, these poisoned waters." He reaches for his box of pins.

"And all that wanders there," adds Ecks. "Great whales and little fishes, killers and narwhals, down to the haddocks and the sponges."

Night falls. They have forgotten to turn on the light, and shadows from the garden, the ancient twisted carob trees, the overgrown bushes, enter the house like uninvited guests.

The Journey, XV: The Lost Paradise

Gordon's arrival at Pueblo de Dios was met with great excitement. Though over the years many foreign and famous, not to say eccentric travellers had come by air or sea—sometimes by the most unexpected means of transport: balloons, galleys, rafts—what distinguished Gordon from the rest was that he had been to the moon.

He spoke of this time and time again, his elbows resting on the tin countertop of the oldest bar in town, from whose roof hung large hams slowly oozing drops of lard. His journey to the moon had lasted five days and five nights (earth time), during which period he had been continuously under the guidance of research centres and monitored by special control towers all over the globe. But all this had taken place years ago and people had forgotten about him, for wonders cannot sustain the full weight of reality. Gordon could not accept that all those people who during the five days of his flight had lived in continuous suspense, who had followed his first steps over the forbidding surface of the moon, who had sent him innumerable congratulatory letters (so many that three full-time secretaries took a year to answer them), that all those people who had prayed for him to return safely to earth, should have so quickly forgotten the adventure, absorbed once again in their daily tasks. What surprised him even more was that the self-same *voyeurs* who had accompanied him (via the TV screen) in his first space walk across the silvery wells of the moon and seen that powdery surface gathered in incredible seas, those craters which hypnotically drew one to their empty depths, could now go on living as before, without that longing to return which dominated his existence.

"Down in the village there's a madman who's been to the moon and now can't find peace," Graciela told Ecks. "He suffers from a nervous disease or something—moonstruck, as the songs say. He's a funny guy, entertaining, if you know how to handle him right. They threw him out or he retired, I don't know. Now he lives here, stays drunk most of the time, and keeps a little bag with him which he says contains moon dust—for all I know it could be his grandad's ashes. You want to meet him? Sometimes he says quite funny things."

At first people gathered around Gordon to listen to him. They would ask him questions. Was it hot or cold on the moon? Did he feel seasick during the journey? What did he eat? Was it true he nearly fell into one of those craters? What vegetation could be made to grow in that soil? Was space transparent? What did the earth look like from out there? What would have happened if he hadn't succeeded? They also wanted to know if he believed in God, if he had nightmares, if he had peed on the moon, how much had they paid him, what did those funny clothes feel like, how many children did he have, and was it true that his wife had cheated on him while he was flying through space?

Time and time again Gordon answered these questions, quoting from his unpublished manuscript narrating his experience, which unfortunately (due to a contract

103

he had signed before the voyage) could not be published without permission from the Department of Space Research, who refused on the grounds of unfair competition with their own publications. In compensation, he was offered on his return the presidency of a bus company called Lunar Trailways Inc., an executive position with an international hotel chain, and a consultancy with a major soft drinks firm which put his portrait in full space regalia on their orangeade. On his return many countries of the world had brought out stamps with his effigy and signature at the bottom. Gordon kept a collection of the first day covers.

Pueblo de Dios could boast other famous residents. There was an important English poet whose books were all out of print. Old and senile, he now sat slumped in a chair, babbling. Some television company had made a popular serial from his one and only novel, and this had enriched his heirs who, nonetheless, never came to see him because they couldn't stand the climate.

There was also a North American physicist who had developed a severe phobia of electricity. He ran away from the research institute where he worked and sought refuge in Pueblo de Dios, where he lived in a house without water or electricity, lit by candles. He was a kind man, very easygoing, so long as one did not use any electrical equipment or display any interest in shavers, blenders or washing machines.

And there was a television comedienne who had retired at the height of her career. She had received a large sum from the channel for which she was working to make a film of her wedding. But at the last minute she ran away from the ceremony—even dropping a satin slipper—and she never returned. The television company sued and she had to return the money. She also had to compensate the groom from her own funds. Some thought it had been the best comic performance of her career. Now she would not allow anybody to mention the word "wedding" in her presence.

Finally there was a famous rapist who had been captured after sowing panic in three cities. When it was found out that he had previously been a policeman, he was quietly released. He then married and came to live in Pueblo de Dios, where he was accepted on condition that he practise his activity outside the town perimeter. Everybody liked him because he had an attractive personality and a gentle nature, and he loved dogs. Lately he had taken to rape again, but only tourists, out of consideration for the locals.

As with these others, Pueblo de Dios got accustomed to Gordon, even got bored with him. He had never gone back to the moon, and his tales were becoming monotonous.

"I so want to go back," he told Ecks in confidence the night they met. "It's the only thing I want in this world."

"In *that* world, you mean"—Ecks clarified. They had been drinking for a while, initiating a careful friendship.

Normally, Gordon did not notice those who listened to him, lost as he was in his own monologue. But this time, perhaps because the bar served a very poor whiskey (more than once he had looked with suspicion at the bottom of his glass, expecting to find a cockroach or other insect) or because Ecks was a new arrival on the island, he actually seemed to pay him some attention:

"By the way," he asked to the other's surprise, "where are you from?" And he looked at Ecks with his grey rat's eyes, the curious, restless eyes of a rat who has gone to the moon and has not yet come back.

"I am an exile," Ecks mumbled, choking in his glass as always, whenever asked a direct question.

"Splendid!" was Gordon's comment. "So you also have been torn away from some place and not allowed to go back. Exile is hard to bear, isn't it, my friend?"

"We have all been exiled from something or someone," urged Ecks in a conciliatory fashion. "I think this is the human condition."

"At night," Gordon continued, "it's always worse at night. I can't stop thinking of that surface, that white surface flattened by my feet. Then, I thought I had so much time. I was bewitched and did not realize time was passing. And what is time after all? When one goes so far away one realizes that it is only a ridiculous convention, an agreement among various parties, a tribal law with mere convenience at its root. I was in no hurry; I walked slowly, taking little steps, not out of fear, but of reverence. Do you understand? I walked slowly as an act of homage; something that the people who looked at us on the screen could never imagine. I had never seen such lakes of ash, such silvery soil. I tell you, my friend, there's no landscape like it. Just imagine the California desert, only up there. Those craters, of all sizes, each one different from the other; I got near them, leaned over, and they seemed to spin around. Could you get an idea from the TV of those craters?" he asked, gulping down the rest of his disgusting whiskey. "When we landed on the moon we toasted with champagne, as on the first sailing of a ship. The other two who came with me were complete non-entities, not at all aware of the romance of our experience; they now spend their time crossing the oceans in yachts full of women. After all, what is the world? The skin of an onion. But those craters!"

"I think I actually fell asleep," confessed Ecks. "You see, the times were bad, dangerous; we were being persecuted and were living in constant fright. That night we could sleep, because, in view of what was happening, we felt sure that even the police would stay at home to watch the television. I did want to watch it too, I wanted to see you, in fact, and I *was* looking at you...I have just realized that you were the man who first got out of the spaceship, held by strings like a puppet, and slowly, but without hesitation, placed your enormous boots on the moon..."

"So, you fell asleep as well?" said Gordon. "I'm not surprised. I'll tell you a secret which has not yet been investigated, though those monsters at the Department of Space Research have forbidden me to talk about it. I'll tell you in all confidence, since we're both exiles and this creates a closer tie than any umbilical cord: millions of people wanted to watch the landing on the moon and were sitting there, waiting with wide open eyes; they knew it was an historical event of the greatest importance and that in years to come their children would ask them how it all happened, and what did the moon look like. Yet, when the moment came, they all fell into a stupor, a form of lethargy. They only woke up when the television cameras stopped transmitting. But you down there weren't the only ones; when I was on the point of landing, I also longed to sleep. I am sure," Gordon went on, "that the moon exercises a sort of hypnotic magnetism which can be felt light-years away."

"German romantic poets like Jean Paul, Richter and others have said something of the kind," commented

Ecks, by now completely drunk.

"Were they astronauts?" Gordon asked sceptically.

"More or less," answered Ecks. "They also travelled."

"I distrust Germans," said Gordon. "They always want to get ahead of the rest, like the Russians. It's the manifestation of an inferiority complex which we study in our courses on Space Psychology."

"A fine subject," said Ecks.

"So you didn't see the craters?" repeated Gordon. The hams hanging from the ceiling were still oozing drops of lard with a slow rhythm which reminded Ecks of the sand in an hour-glass.

"Of what substance were they? Stone?" Ecks inquired for politeness' sake.

"I don't know." Gordon had suddenly become sad. "We were not able to examine anything closely at the time. Like animals of prey we were only able to steal and take away, take and steal. The analyses were done later in those numberless laboratories of the different sections of the Department, numberless like the cells in a bee-hive... We were the bees."

"Where did you suck?" Ecks was becoming interested.

"In the beautiful craters. Do belly-buttons turn you on?"

"Somewhat," answered Ecks noncommittally.

"The most beautiful belly-buttons I've ever seen."

"Of what substance were they?" Ecks was now quite taken by the idea.

"There on the moon one forgets everything, my friend. The pangs of love, the space budget, the rent due, the childrens' education, everything... Even death."

Gordon sounded solemn, and Ecks thought this was the proper state of mind for an astronaut, for a man who has glimpsed the beauty of space and has been forever deprived of it, condemned from then on to wander over the crowded earth in eternal longing.

"The terrible thing is not being able to go back," said the astronaut.

"It has been said (was it Virgil or Horace?) that we always leave the place where we could be forever happy," Ecks offered.

"At first I didn't think I would feel so heartsick," said Gordon, who was no longer listening. "I was too excited and fascinated by it all. That silence...because there is hardly any sound out there. But it is a silence one can hear; just a few almost imperceptible sounds like that of a nut rolling to the ground, a breeze crackling, or the beat of a firefly's wings. It frightens you at first, because it is a silence which *occupies* space, if you take my meaning. It extends in its vacuum. And in order to understand the relation between this silence and the immensity of space you need to retreat and collect your thoughts. After a while you grow to love it. Finally you can't live without it: it becomes the only possible habitat. I had to divorce my wife because she was jealous, and she was right. Women don't attract me any more. I have only one desire: to reconstruct, to relive that experience. The film of the journey that the Space Research Center gave me—I've seen it over and over again—but it's no use to me. My own memories are infinitely more beautiful. Why couldn't I stay there? I'm lost on earth. These cars, houses, crowds, noises... What are they compared with that surface hard as ice, yet which one feels must be soft and tender (no, those aren't the right words) beneath. Those leaden deserts... Do you know the moon is full of seas and deserts? Not our kind of seas and deserts; something else, something you can't describe because in order to do so you can only use the images one is familiar with, while the moon participates in another order. Like God.

"The worst of it all," he rumbled on, lost in his thoughts, "is to know that I shall never go back. Do you understand? *Never again*. Isn't it terrible? To see her from afar and know that I shall never get near her again. They won't send back someone who has been there already. Besides they don't trust me now. I have put on too much weight, drink too much, am divorced, have no job and talk too much. A bad space traveller: one who never got over the experience."

"Is there a technical term for this?" asked Ecks.

"*Space psychosis*," muttered Gordon and asked for more whiskey.

Hopelessly drunk, Ecks and Gordon remained in the bar for many hours, until the owner, tired of listening to them, threw them out. He wanted to tend to his hams and was rather annoyed with them: he didn't like to hear his whiskey maligned on his own premises.

They went out together—the night was filled with the perfume of the lavender fields—and crossed the village on the way to the beach, talking of things which nobody and perhaps not even they themselves would understand. They walked past the pharmacy and the owner's wife, wakened by their voices, grumbled that voyaging to the moon does not improve some people's manners. Next they reached the bakery where the baker, also awakened, shouted that some people were exiled with good reason; the trouble was they ended up on somebody else's doorstep. Gordon threw a stone at his window but missed. "Ever since I came back," he explained to Ecks, "I've had difficulty assessing the true weight of objects. Out in space it was so different."

"Of course," slurred Ecks, "loss of gravity."

On the corner stood a gasoline pump. Gordon pointed and laughed, "There are still people who travel on that stuff!" Ecks informed him that he preferred to travel on foot. "Yes," agreed Gordon, "when your foot rests on the unknown, your body quivers with metaphysical excitement." Ecks liked the sound of this phrase.

Falling down from time to time, they reached the shore. The night was deep and starless. The sand was deserted, not a boat was tied up; there was no wind, the rocks were silhouetted in the distance. In the sky the moon shone, round and majestic, full of white light, in the silence which was only broken by the soft sound of the waves.

"There she is," shouted Gordon, who began to run down the beach like an excited child. He was looking at her from all angles, changing position to see her better, searching for her seas and her lakes, her mercury deserts and her magnetic craters, her opaque fields and deep wells.

"Isn't she beautiful?" he asked Ecks, breathless with desire.

It occurred to Ecks that there are journeys from which one cannot return.

By the side of the pilgrim Angel of Light, in the segment to the right set in symmetry to the one previously described, there is another circle. Represented in it is a man's head ending in flames and the word Sun; next to it in a smaller circle, a woman's head on which rests the dial of the moon. There are also stars, conventionally represented, and the phrase Ubi dividit Deus aquas ab aquis *(And God divided the waters from the waters). Among the stars can be seen, in abbreviation, the word* firmamentum.

In the lower part of the tapestry, in the segment which occupies most space, beneath the figure of the Creator with his hand raised in blessing, is displayed the world of birds and fishes. One can read the inscriptions volatilia celi *(birds of the sky) and* cete grandis *(great fishes). The birds are not very different from real ones; they appear with open wings on the point of taking flight; their beaks are short and triangular; they are all looking up towards the sky (which coincides with the circle of the Creator) and their bodies are lithe and agile. Under the birds, without any dividing line between sea and the sky, swim the fishes, both great and small. There is a sea-worm, coiled up, with a black head pointing upwards; other aquatic animals are represented with less realism. One has a dog's head and a snake's body, under a large red shell provided with two small wings. Another has the head of a crocodile, donkey's ears, and fins. They occupy a large area of this section of the tapestry, as if sea-monsters were the most important part of creation.*

Ship-captains and sailors of the past were those who best knew the universe—the skies, waters and lands— who could tell the world what the world was like, know its myths and keep its legends. Their memories—and at times their journals—were the source of knowledge and the means of its diffusion. When one wanted to know the name of an exotic plant, the use of certain herbs, the customs of certain animals, the constellations appearing on specific routes, the origin of a word and of many of the images which illustrate the thought and fantasies of antiquity, it was to these journals that one referred. Centuries later, when the skies, the seas and the land began to lose their mystery and the imagination and fears of men turned on each other—a neighbour being more frightening than a nocturnal animal or a general more dangerous than a flooding river—the ancient prestige and function of these salty travellers faded. They stopped writing and their main tasks became trade and war. Their memories no longer captivated the attention of those who did not travel. Their journeys are now shorter and safer. But also less interesting.

It is probable that the anonymous weaver of the tapestry (if indeed there was only one) knew, from descriptions by the old sea captains and sailors, of the marvellous monsters which (according to them) inhabited the seas, only to be glimpsed in the lightning's flash or in terror as the mast came crashing down. Scarcely separate from the roiling sea and its menace, these creatures were never seen to wander far from their deep-sea caves. Though each unexpected apparition sowed panic, there was always a brave sailor ready to thrust his harpoon into the whirling waters, his figure—like one possessed—etched against the darkness of the night.

The sea monsters of the tapestry do not inspire fear. They join harmoniously in the great system of creation, together with the birds and plants. Strange-looking creatures they are, but their extraordinary appearance does not terrify, any more than do those gentle monstrosities, the Anfisbena *or* Mirmecoleón. *They seem to glide naturally through the waves with no apparent desire of emerging or attacking, and beside them, unthreatened, swim the smaller fishes.*

XVI: Morris, A Journey To The Earth's Navel

Life went on as usual: Ecks fished in the contaminated waters of the sea, not daring to eat what he caught for fear of sulfuric acid; Morris was bringing to an end his research on the life cycle of Lepidoptera in mountainous regions; Graciela was working on a study of ancient deflowering rituals; Stanley, the house dog, pursued cats and other intruders (mainly visitors) and Felix, the talking parrot, rythmically repeated the verse which Ecks had taught him: *Vegno del loco onde tornar disio* ("I come from where I wish to return"). This line, apparently, had been pronounced by none other than Beatrice herself, long before the metropolis' poets had started their navel-gazing. Nobody had the delicacy to ask the parrot where he wished to return, though Morris assured them it was the Amazonian jungle.

Then, unexpectedly, a letter from the metropolis, whose writing could not be identified as any of the habitual correspondents of Morris, was delivered into his hands. It invited him to undertake a journey to the Great Navel for reasons which were to his advantage, though, given the date of the letter, he wondered whether these reasons still applied.

To undertake a journey to the Great Navel was a delicate business for Morris: he was accustomed to a peaceful life, all the more so since even his trips to the post office had been suspended now that Graciela and Ecks were collecting his mail.

That very night preparations for the big event began. Morris was excited and nervous. Umbilical matters terrified him and he could not leave anything to chance.

"Let's make a detailed plan of all my movements through the labyrinth," he told his friends, scattering over the tables various sheets of paper and maps of different sizes. The relevant geographical features, routes and possible dangers were marked.

The first question was what means of transport should be used. A boat was immediately excluded because Morris was terrified of shipwrecks, could not swim, and his grandfather (never before had Graciela heard about this grandfather) had died in a nautical accident. "On the *Titanic*," stated Morris, faced with general incredulity.

On the other hand, Morris objected to aeroplanes, since he hated the sound of engines and suffered from claustrophobia; when he was inside a plane, all he wanted was for it to crash so he could get back into the open.

"I should like to go on horseback, or on foot...I don't see why we have stopped using the horse as a means of transport. It may be a little slow, but it is immensely more human. Moreover I get airsick," lamented Morris.

"Since we no longer make use of horses," Graciela advised, "the only solution is to go by air. I have some travel-sickness pills: you can take one tonight and one tomorrow just before the flight."

The pills were carefully examined:

"I detest having to introduce unknown chemicals into the delicate metabolism of my guts and glands," protested Morris, "But I detest even more feeling sick," and he proceeded to swallow one.

The parrot shrieked *Vegno del loco onde tornar disio* and Morris thought of taking him along for company in the Great Navel, but one could only bring animals in a cage onto an aeroplane and Felix had often told Morris that he too suffered from claustrophobia.

The next question was what to wear. Morris did not like to attract attention, he only wished to go unnoticed in the cities; yet at times excess of sobriety in attire had exactly the opposite effect.

"In a blue suit, waistcoat, white shirt, grey tie and black shoes you will inevitably become very conspicuous," warned Graciela. "You will be an unidentifiable object walking through the streets. People will turn and look at you, wonder whether you come from some period of the past and ask whether you have ever met any of their ancestors."

Morris was horrified.

"You'd better wear a shirt with red stripes ("Awful!") and a leather jacket."

"Never!" he shouted, "leather irritates my skin."

"Better a bout of eczema than your nervous system in shreds."

"All right," Morris capitulated. "A fragile plane will take me to the Great Navel, unless it first crashes, burns in the air and falls into the contaminated waters of a river; or loses a wing or an engine, as planes are apt to do. But the Great Navel, as you will see from this map"—and he unfolded one full of blue and red lines—"has a very complex structure: there converge (I shall never know whether they come or go) wide avenues, all alike, crowded with shops, restaurants, offices, travel and real estate agents, banks, ballet schools, discotheques, beauty parlours, saunas, hairdressers, cabinetmakers and bars."

"And houses," whispered Graciela.

"That's the worst," answered Morris. "Buildings, apartments, one on top of the other in unbearable promiscuity. All alike so that one seems to be in one place when one is somewhere else. Once I opened a door, interrupting a cosy family meal. The father, an honest man, reliable worker etc., thought I was a thief and threw a dish of hot soup in my face. It was fish soup. I had mistaken the door; I lived in an identical building next to his, on the same floor bearing the same number and having the same disposition of rooms. It is very difficult to get the smell of fish out of one's clothes... Well, once in the metropolis, I have to find 386 Albion Street, as the letter indicates."

"You'd better take a taxi," suggested Ecks.

"Impossible," answered Graciela. "He won't find an empty one. He doesn't know the ways of the jungle."

"Taxis?" asked Morris. "Those revolting two-toned objects with four legs, driven by swearing neurotics, where the passengers are seen at prayer?"

"Perhaps he can take the metro," wondered Ecks, consulting the map.

"I shall never go in one of those machines," Morris protested. "They make too much noise so you can't hear what people say; besides they are always packed with soldiers on their day off who bellow at each station. They're dark, unhealthy, and the automatic doors don't work. I remember when I was a child I saw a woman trapped: I could only see one leg, one arm and one of her breasts, while those waiting on the platform were able to appreciate the other half; there seemed to be no way to bring the two together. People were screaming and so I imagine was the poor woman. It was horrible. One of her shoes fell off. Finally some fellow-travellers began to pull her from inside and those on the platform began to do the same from the outside. People in the other compartments were complaining of the delay: they wanted the filthy machine to carry on its way with or without the other half of the woman. They were late, their children were expecting them; besides they had paid their fares to go to such and such a station and not to watch a tug-of-war. I shall never go that way again!"

"We might find a bus which goes in the right direction," offered Graciela, patiently checking the map.

"Remember," Ecks warned her, "that the names of the streets have changed since the last government."

"I belong to the old government!" answered Morris, suddenly conservative from fear of travelling.

"I think I shall walk there," he finally added. "I shall try not to look either to right or left. Just stare ahead."

"It's a bit far," Ecks said. "We'll have to draw up a plan for you."

"I have never been able to orient myself in cities," warned Morris. "I don't believe that cardinal points exist there or, if they do, they keep on shifting."

Together Graciela and Ecks worked out a detailed plan full of arrows and points of reference for Morris to follow.

"I could always walk dropping small pebbles every few steps," he observed. "Like those obnoxious children in fairy tales with which the famous intellectuals of the Great Navel like to identify nowadays. There is something obscene in an adult proclaiming his affinity with Pinocchio, Wendy or Snow White."

"Watch your words," Ecks warned. "The Great Navel does not forgive; it persecutes dissidents."

120

Appendix

The Metropolis According to Morris

The principal occupation of the city's inhabitants is staring at their navels. However, they are not aware of it: buried in one of its most hidden folds which ramifies and spreads into multiple creases, they have completely forgotten that they are in the depths of a navel and not in the real world at all. They give many and varied names to their activity, but they cannot be accused of hypocrisy or insincerity, because one of the characteristics of spending all ones time staring at one's navel is exactly this: that one doesn't know that all one is staring at is a piece of useless flesh.

The Navel-gazing operation implies being inside and not outside the navel, with the result that only those who do not contemplate their navel can see those who do, which leads to a state of complete isolation.

By contemplating their navels all day, the city's inhabitants are kept fully occupied and have no time left to worry about what may happen in the world outside. There is for instance the matter of the folds: each citizen who thoroughly examines his navel (and all the citizens of B. do so) is well aware of its number of folds, one different from the other in shape, depth, height, width and texture. Some navels have deep folds which gather dirt, while others with quite shallow folds remain generally clean. Now, the study of each minute crease, its course, its cracks and lines requires a lot of time; there is also the question of the many possible accidents which can occur, like the man who was smothered in a fold or the woman who choked on fluff. He who becomes involved with one of these creases knows when he enters but not

121

when he will come out.

Thoroughly engrossed in studying the structure of each fold, exploring all its creases, the citizens of B. have an image of the world as of a circular enclosure, of which they are the main inhabitants, as students and masters of the umbilical. The smallest defect in shape, colour or texture becomes the subject of grave discussion : Should the navel be cleaned with soap or dusted with talcum? Should it be protected or remain uncovered? Are twenty-seven creases preferable to twenty-one? Are square-shaped navels more ancient than rounded ones? What kind of profession fits better with a clean navel and what is the best system of navel irrigation? Political parties are impotent when faced with the great problems of the world, being altogether absorbed in pronouncing judgement on the various polemics on navels and in the debates raging among the three factions. There are those who belong to the center-umbilical party, who maintain that all folds must blossom out from a pivotal point; members of the left-umbilical party, on the other hand, hold that the folds on the left are more important, since this is the side where the vital organs of the body are to be found; while the rightists insist on the need to establish the supreme authority of Navelism by eliminating all those imperfect in shape, slightly left-of-centre, hairy, squinting, less than rosebud-size.

The navel industry occupies a large part of the life of the citizens of B., creating active and prosperous businesses of which they are rightly proud, and arousing the envy of their neighbours who spend their life contemplating their eye-sockets. It is a domestic industry in which all the family participate though, this being a patriarchal society, the father is in control. Such a system has the usual disadvantages, because the faults of the parents—laziness, meanness, selfishness and vanity—are passed on both by example and inclination. Each navel is a factory, just as each family is an industry. Though they are a maritime people, their "navelist" vision of the world has not expanded: when they travel, they do so within one of the folds of the navel, taking great care not to step out of it. However, the citizens of B. are convinced that they are the most cultured and patriotic people in the world. This conviction spurs them on to further study of their navels. They are not aware that the citizens of C., who spend their time contemplating their feet, believe exactly the same, as do the citizens of Y., who are entirely dedicated to listening to their ears by a system of echoing mirrors. "It could be that navel industry is not very aesthetic," they admit at times, "but it is very beneficial and favours the growth of our city."

The newspapers, reviews, books and films which appear in B. are all navel-inspired. They deal with phenomena occurring within navels, observed and studied through microscopes. Prizes are awarded to the best descriptive and illustrative works, thus stimulating the growth and perfecting the quality of navelist art and literature. The best navel poets always start their works with the word *I*, as do their novelists. In these texts we read abundantly of the authors' navel vicissitudes, how they love, cherish and will never leave their navels.

The Great Navel has a more-or-less oval shape, from whatever angle it may be viewed. Those who enter there, as if in the depths of a mine, find their way out with difficulty. Trapped like flies, in vain they stretch their limbs or wave their antennae: the viscid folds impede their escape. On the outskirts of the place grow trees and other plants beside the banks of running streams, but factory smoke thickens the air and covers everything with a patina of grey.

Though one navel is much like the next, each inhabitant is convinced of the utter uniqueness of his own. Entire books have been published on the differences, both descriptive essays and original research; and as each person chooses to read only what pertains to his own habitat, the fallacy of uniqueness is not only confirmed, but increased. Great pains are taken to point out the different depths of each navel, the special design and complex network of folds. Navel genealogy forms an important branch of study, as does research into the morphology of navels and their adaptation throughout history.

But life is not pleasant here. Though navelists insist—not without humour—that they have reached the peak of civilization, this is clearly untenable, even a lie. The streets smell in winter as in summer, no plants grow, buildings crumble and timetables go unobserved. The poor beg in the crevices, homeless children and neglected old people. Mad navelists can be seen wandering at all hours of the day, immersed in their delusions.

A navel moves subtly in various directions. These spasmodic contractions can be taken for activity, but a careful analysis of the comings and goings, motions and commotions leads to the conclusion that not all movement signifies change or progress. What they describe as movement is in fact no more than convulsion. Throughout its spasms the Navel remains dirty and smelly. Moreover it is horribly noisy. Decibels reach the top of the scale: cars, trucks and motorbikes, steamrollers turbines and cranes, buses, trains above and below ground, polishers, electric saws and other machinery, mothers and children, all create a continuous roar, so that when one needs to speak one must shout. With the result that conversation among navelists increases in pitch to such an extent that one opens one's mouth and strains one's vocal chords in vain. This leads to a lack of communication and the need for psychoanalists.

Cultural life in the Great Navel does not offer much variety; famous citizens edit their memoirs before dying; only, having passed their lives contemplating their navels, their memoirs are remarkably alike; having read one, one has read them all. Besides, they do not contain amusing anecdotes; each merely describes what the navel looked like years ago and how time passed inside it; how navels were inherited, settled, and the various things found within their folds. Always the same story, the same as one tells one's friends, and frankly quite boring. If they could stop looking at their navels, they might be more interesting, but they are far too busy classifying all the crevices, mounts and wells...

The favourite animal among navelists is the car, which they value above any family member. This inseparable companion enjoys the protection of its master and the attention of experts. Some navelists won't even leave it behind when they go to the supermarket.

XVII: What Happened to Morris in Albion

In the Great Navel Morris suffers from watering eyes, blocked nose, muscle cramps, and a heavy head as though he were wearing a helmet. Whenever he enters one of those enormous multi-storied department stores where one can buy anything from a needle to a yacht, chewing gum to garden gnomes, he falls under a spell. He wanders like an automaton beneath the metallic fluorescent lights, among crowded stalls and counters, up and down escalators, unable to find the exit. And all he wanted to buy was a handkerchief, having forgotten to bring one along.

The marble sign with elegant purple lettering said *Albion Publishers*. Morris pushed open the door and went in. Along the corridor were numerous cubicles surrounded by glass screens; inside them, clerks of both sexes. Some gave him indifferent glances before continuing with their work.

This is the way the Great Navel acknowledges one's presence, thought Morris, as he sat waiting in one of the uncomfortable chairs lined up against the main wall. Everybody seemed very busy; telephones rang without being answered, and this added to the general sense of feverish activity. That's the way it is in the Great Navel, he thought; people are so occupied that they cannot be

126

interrupted for any reason. One has to wait until they can be interrupted, so that they may become occupied once more. All the magazines which lay on the occasional table in front of Morris were pornographic and therefore monotonous. He felt no desire to look at them.

Finally, a door opened. A young woman whose face was as impassive outside the glass screen as from inside, stepped half-heartedly in his direction. Morris immediately stood up.

"What can I do for you?" she asked; neutral voice determined to cut out any contact.

Morris swallowed hard, cursed the day and probably the days to come, the lifeless neon lights of the office, the banal songs fed through the radio, the monotonous hammering of typewriters and the symmetry of the mosaic on the walls.

"You see," he muttered, "I have written a book."

"You are not the only one," she answered brutally. "I imagine you are looking for a publisher. They all are. If you want us to have a look at it—-without any commitment on our part, of course—you must first fill in this form," and she extracted a paper from the file under her arm. "Once you have answered our questions, you can hand in your manuscript, retaining a copy for yourself. We will be in touch with you within a certain period of time which could be anything between two weeks and a year. We are very busy; every day the number of authors increases and the number of readers diminishes. We do not hold ourselves responsible for your manuscript; therefore only complete the form if you have a copy in your house or hotel bedroom."

Morris agreed. The woman brandished the form in her hands like a weapon; Morris wondered what crime he had committed; some crime of which he was unaware, as is often the case—mistakes, accidents, chance happenings, which we forget, perhaps in order not to assume responsibility. But the law does not forgive. The law, the young woman from the publishing house, the bank, the universe, never forgive.

Looking at him severely, the woman handed him the form and added:

"I'll stay here while you fill it in. If you have any queries, do not hesitate to consult me." And she proceded to look at some papers.

Morris began to fill in the form: name, nationality, place of birth, qualifications, the colour of his eyes and hair, his present address, telephone number and the number of his bank account.

1. *Description of the work*. To what genre does it belong? a) Novel b) Short story c) Essay d) Poem.

Morris hesitated. He held the pen in the air and the woman stared at him.

"The fact is," he explained, "I am not sure whether I can answer the first question. I don't know whether my work is a short novel, a long story or a narrative essay. It is just a piece of prose, with some poetic fragments, to be exact, perhaps an epic... Do you follow me?"

"This house only publishes novels, stories, poems and essays," the woman insisted. "Either one or the other."

"This seems to me a lamentable simplification," protested Morris. "Epic and poetry have merged from time immemorial, as have realism and fantasy. Think of the Song of Roland, or the Saga of the Nibelungs, not to mention the Homeric poems..."

"One or the other," the woman went on implacably.

Morris resigned himself. There is a secret subtle mechanism which ensures that the more one is oppressed the more repressive one becomes. Who had thought of this? Freud or Marx?

2. *Summarize in ten lines the content of the work.*

Morris thought a while without writing.

"I cannot describe the content of four hundred pages in a few meagre lines," he declared. "How can one express all the nuances...?"

"All the questions on the form must be answered," she interrupted him unforgivingly.

Morris wrote:

Practical instruction on how to get lost in the city. Traffic regulations. Description of public footpaths. How to avoid cancer, learn German in three weeks. The work deals with everything. Of the whole in its multiple aspects. That is, of the whole in its infinitesimal particles. In it one reads episodes from the life of Sir Lancelot, how to eliminate ants from the garden, the life cycle of Lepidoptera in the Epanurus Mountains, the resonances of classical mythology in French cooking, Aztec rites, and six methods for preserving chastity used in ancient Rome.

3. *What predominates in your work? Action? Sex? Politics?*

Morris looked at the woman and explained:

"My book is predominantly metaphysical, to use a traditional classification. Although it is not a late exposition of Aristotelianism, nor yet can it be defined as Thomist. What do I put down?"

The woman sighed. Writers were like children.

"Is there any action in your work?" she asked patiently.

"Yes, you might say so," answered Morris, "if you

consider that the mere fact of being a *work* implies the action of elaborating a product, even though it may not be edible nor even (probably) consumable. Can one deny that there is an action, a slow painful action, full of obstacles, and, perhaps, given the present times, gratuitous?''

"If that is the case, write that in your book action predominates,'' calmly advised the woman.

"As for sex,'' went on Morris, "the form does not specify. Is there a priviliged sex?''

This question seemed to interest the woman more.

"Generally speaking,'' she informed him, "I can tell you that a work of female sex has very little chance of success, unless it is purely and clearly a sentimental story. We publish very few works of female sex, which is not surprising, since there aren't that many written. The public demands masculine works, as do the critics. Women readers also prefer masculine works, such is the trend of our civilization.''

"I think my book is androgynous,'' Morris confessed melancholically.

She looked at him with some tenderness. Without meaning to, Morris had awakened her maternal instinct. He always seemed to have this effect on women. Perhaps it was his red hair; he had read somewhere that many women dreamed of having red-haired sons, perhaps because in films and television serials red-haired boys were clever, attractive, good-natured.

"Are you serious?'' her tone was sympathetic.

Morris began to feel slightly guilty; a guilt which grew and began to manifest itself throughout his body up to the tips of his red hair. But this time his guilt seemed to melt into a sea of milk, it was well-received and rocked in a female lap...

130

"Yes," he muttered. "I really think my book is androgynous."

"You could see a doctor," she insinuated protectively. "You mustn't worry too much. Relax and think of other things. I know of many cases like yours. It is not up to me to suggest, but why don't you put down that your book is of masculine sex?. Then at least they'll look at it. Sometimes it's better to tell a little lie."

"But this would be betraying the deep essence, the very nature of the work, attributing to it a sex it doesn't have!"

"And so what?" she asked in a conciliatory voice. "Don't we all attribute ourselves a sex? And spend our lives proving it? Do you realize, we waste our lives trying to convince others—and ourselves—that we have a sex, with its specific identity, which we use and suitably embellish and display."

"Yes," Morris said. "It seems a neurotic preoccupation. What does it matter in the end?"

"That's it; the end of sex is neurosis. It drives our lives. But since those are rules of the game, let's accept them: from now on your book is of masculine sex. Any politics there?" she asked.

Morris thought.

"In the more general sense of the word, yes, there are politics in my book. Since man stopped living alone in caves, because of the humidity, everything has become political, don't you think? But, going back to what you said before, if it is neurotic to be preoccupied with one sex, isn't it also neurotic to be preoccupied with one system of politics?"

"I think," the woman answered, "that the fact that we talk more and more about politics is precisely due to

131

the lack of it. Haven't you noticed, for example, how everybody feels a compulsion to eat potatoes just when the crop has failed? The same phenomenon."

"Only with the difference," added Morris, "that, as history moves—backwards, forwards or sideways, as the case may be—the sexes are multiplying: didn't Lawrence Durrell talk, years ago, of the six sexes of Alexandria? Whereas in politics the opposite happens: the range of political registers of which we seem capable diminishes all the time, like a piano which is losing its keys. Nowadays there are but two politics and the differences between the two are minimal. It is easy to pass from one to the other; you can spend the first half of your life proclaiming the principles of one and acting according to the other and the second half inverting the order. This is what is called ideological fluidity."

4. *Do you think that your book will be commercially profitable?*

Without consulting the woman, Morris wrote: "As profitable as soap or as electric mixers; it depends on the methods of marketing."

5. *Is it an optimistic or a pessimistic book?*

Morris shivered with disgust as he did every time he came across these words.

"I find the fifth question completely unnecessary," he told the woman. "By the mere fact that it exists, every book is optimistic, assuming that this damnable word means something."

"Don't you believe it," she answered. "I would argue the exact opposite. The abundance of manuscripts indicates general pessimism: it shows that nothing is right in the world. And don't forget that a third of the world population is illiterate and therefore unable even to write

132

down its complaints. Put down that your work is moderately optimistic; that's the best answer and does not commit anybody. You can always show that there is a certain amount of optimism in your work, if only in the dedication."

Morris was exhausted. He finished filling in the form and gave it to the woman. This brought him a certain elation.

"Would you come out and have a drink with me after work?" he asked the woman.

"I'm sorry," she answered. "We're not allowed to go out with writers. The senior editor says neurosis is catching."

In the segment on the right between the Sun (the man with his head surrounded by flames) and Moon (the woman with the moondial on her forehead), and the world of birds and fishes, appears Adam. He is naked, bearded, and is calling the animals by name. The legend below says: Adam non inveniebatur similem sibi *(Adam did not find his like).*

In the tapestry the figure of Adam (on a background of green threads) rises from a land strewn with flowers. Around him various animals receive their verbal baptism. But we do not know by what name he addressed the small winged reptile with a striped body to his left, nor what name he gave to the horse with a tiger's head or the winged deer. For Adam was very alone (he still had not found his like).

Only the plants and those curious-looking animals were there to receive his words.

The Journey, XVIII: A Knight of the Holy Grail

Percival went to the lake and looked at the empty soda containers floating in the water. Funny word, *container*, he thought, imagining other containers which also went on water, but looked different. His mind did not linger long on this reflection; he was looking for his favourite ducks amidst the floating debris. They normally appeared gliding through the dirty papers, the plastic bottles and the crumpled cigarette packs, moving with dignity as though, thought Percival, they were deliberately ignoring the litter which soiled the lake and converted it into a fetid dump. He watched them come from behind the reeds, swimming gracefully, manoeuvring around the garbage flung from the shores, accepting pollution as inevitable.

Percival could not understand why people treated the lake as though it were a rubbish tip; actually at times he did understand it—which was even worse—and became angry and wanted to attack the whole world. The ducks lost their glamour and became sad, decrepit birds, beggars, hardly able to survive in the crowded lake; the water turned oily and slimy; the transparent fish no longer flickered beneath.

Percival looked at the faded signs which forbade walking on the grass, throwing litter and disturbing the birds. Twisted and uprooted by storms, these posts looked like desolate scarecrows which had lost their function.

Nobody seemed to know the name of the trees in the park; at least none of the people Percival had asked. He would point to a branch, a trunk, the delicate structure of a leaf without success. Passersby faced with his inquiry stared round with curiosity, as though noticing for the first time that this was a park full of trees. Pressed, they would answer vaguely that perhaps that was a privet or an auracaria, and that there were definitely some magnolias. Nobody ever gave him the name of a plant with assurance. This applied to the occasional visitors; as for those Percival knew by sight—those who came as regularly as he did—they walked silently with their heads down, absorbed in their deepest thoughts and isolated from the world. They were mainly men. Percival wondered why they came; no doubt there was some obscure reason, deeply hidden in their minds, which neither their faces nor their gestures betrayed.

He, on the other hand, had many good reasons for coming here. First of all there were the ducks; something in their appearance gave him a sensation of harmony and kinship. Looking at them he was overcome by a kind of hypnosis which transported him into a past, unknown and unremembered, yet definitely real. He did not know what he had been in that remote past, but he felt a strong affinity with the lake and the ducks. He had probably been some shapeless substance; that's what it was, he had been a substance related to water and ducks; that was why whenever he looked at them now, that comforting feeling of kinship returned.

The second reason why Percival liked to come to

the park was the bandstand in the centre. It was an old circular kiosk with a handsome dome which rose to a thin spire; this produced in him a sensation similar to the one caused by the ducks. The stand had once been surrounded by glass; time and hail stones had shattered it and the sides now gaped open. These decaying structures seemed beautiful to Percival, with that rare beauty of things which survive only in part, empty, unable to function. (His mother had once described this as an aspect of decadence; he did not understand the meaning of the word, but he liked it because, he explained, it sounded connected with time. More he couldn't say; whenever he thought of time, he felt uneasy, as though something strange and disturbing were happening to him. Yet he was sure that all beautiful decadent things were so because of their connection with time.)

Under the dome stood the musicians' chairs. They didn't exactly stand; that is, one could not see them, they had lost their tangible appearance, but they were undoubtedly there, and whenever one gazed in that direction, one became aware of their presence. They existed in the mind, in their logical place. And they had really been there, once. Percival's mother had told him that when she was a little girl she went to musical evenings in the park. The musicians took their place on the podium under the cover of the dome on finely carved wooden chairs arranged in a semicircle. After the concert, his mother had told him, she would walk in the park holding her parents' hands.

"And the chairs, did they remain there?" asked Percival. His mother made an effort to remember, but was not able to answer him with surety. She assumed that they did until the park-keeper came and took them inside the shed next to the public toilets.

But all this had come to an end. One day, the concerts stopped, the orchestra was disbanded. But what happened to the chairs? Percival liked to think that they remained there under the domed roof, exposed to the elements, and that bit by bit they broke down and disintegrated, until they disappeared, leaving the place empty.

Grass sprouted from the frame, licking the edge of the stage. The children picked at the loose floor tiles, leaving concrete scars. The stand had now become the meeting place of doves. They came from all over and perched there on the railings, or lined up in order and symmetry on the dome. Their profiles, etched against the grey purplish sky of twilight, looked like stone images, gargoyles on a cathedral.

From time to time, in order to break up that symmetry which annoyed him a little—and only for this reason—Percival threw stones at them. The doves then rose and circled, pretending to leave their perches, but soon returned. Percival felt that the birds gathered there to perform a rite, belonging to a secret cult unknown to him, and he resented feeling excluded.

Whenever he was caught by the rain (rain often came down in the afternoons like a delicate curtain over the solitary park), Percival took shelter in the bandstand. But he would find himself alone, because the doves for some mysterious reason seemed to disappear, perhaps trying to keep dry under the eaves and the roofs of nearby houses. From his pavilion Percival looked out at the rain, a solitary god at the centre of creation. The wet trunks of the trees glittered; the fallen leaves swirled in the wind; the surface of the lake bristled with small whirlpools.

From the edge of the stage, he watched the willows incline their slender, translucent branches; the poplars shake their leaves, whipped from side to side; while the magic effects of occasional lightning zigzagged through the sky. The few visitors ran away, abandoning the park like a battlefield suddenly hit by a meteor, and leaving behind a trail of waste: flimsy paper bags festively flying in the air, and wet pages of newspapers, their sad news washed away in the rain. The empty cans lay on the grass like the last grenades of a lost war, and the stalls for cold drinks and ice cream were hidden under nylon covers on which the rain formed lakes in perfect scale.

Percival was the only one to shelter in the old band-stand, and he felt that it belonged to him: that ancient proprietary right of scouts, discoverers and lovers. He might only just have permitted his mother to join him there, but no one else.

Under the rain which filled the gaps in the ground, and the lightning which cut the slate-coloured sky with its mysterious splendour, Percival experienced again a sense of the past. It seemed perfectly natural to be there below the dome, watching the solitude of the rain, the bristling of the lake surface; it corresponded to some other primitive sensation which he carried in his genes, even though the memory of it had faded.

This is why he was extremely surprised when that evening he found somebody else under the dome. He spotted him from afar, as he left the shore of the lake where he had been watching the ducks. Percival had not taken them bread, nor had he talked to them. Leaning on the iron railings scarred with rust, he had gazed fascinated at them sliding past, had felt the water under his body, had swum with them to the island, wondering at the equilibrium and fusion which were naturally maintained between lake and ducks. As the shadows of the cypress trees lengthened on the water, he had turned towards the bandstand.

He saw the silhouette of the stranger erect in the middle of the podium, a dark shape which desecrated his temple. He hesitated and thought of going once more to the lake, where the ducks continued swimming unperturbed. If he met with something which he did not like, he was in the habit of ignoring it for a while and resuming previous activities, to give destiny a chance to rearrange the infinite chain of events which had resulted in a specific reality. If he turned around—as if he hadn't seen that intruder who had dared place himself in the middle of the bandstand—and went back to the lake and the ducks, perhaps sequences would re-shape themselves in a different pattern and when he next went to the bandstand, the man would not be there and everything would go back to normal. Possibly destiny had not made a mistake; he had confused the hour. Only a few more moments with the ducks and the intruder would be gone, and it would be as if he had never been there. When suddenly a stone falls on the head of a passerby, it is not the fault of destiny, but of the victim who has miscalculated his timing. The merit of having been until now the only occupier of the place lay exactly in his ability to understand time. Only this once he had made a mistake; he had chosen the wrong moment to go there and had lost his power. Now, on the other hand, it would have been wrong to go back to the ducks as if it was not his mistake; he had to assume his responsibility and face the new situation.

The man was relatively young (which for Percival

meant younger than thirty); he had reddish hair and full lips. Percival tried to control himself; his irritation grew by the moment. When he drew near he circled the place as if it were not his final target. He often used guerrilla strategies to confront the various manifestations of adult power. Some he had acquired intuitively, being a child and therefore one of the oppressed. Others he had learnt from books or from talking with grown-ups who remembered episodes of their own struggles. He picked up a stone which was not bothering anybody and threw it far away; pulled a few strands of grass, sniffed one, bit it and then spat it out; followed the path of some ants; put together empty bottles which might come in handy as weapons. Finally he mounted the stand.

Morris had been looking at the child with curiosity. He must have been eight or nine years old; his pale fine hair hardly covered his earlobes; he was slender; thin legs emerged from a pair of short trousers of indescribable colour. But what most attracted Morris were his eyes. They were the colour of ash but by no means spent; green and blue sparks flashed the irises giving them extraordinary vivacity. He moved with ease and agility like an acrobat or, rather, a ballet dancer. He seemed to have complete control of all muscles, tendons and tissues of his body; more than that, Morris guessed that the child possessed another kind of control which he exercised over the order of the world around him.

"Good afternoon," Morris said in order to break the ice. "I am Morris. I'm feeling a little tired; if you don't mind I would like to rest here a while. This is a very good spot and it has a lovely view."

The boy looked at him showing no sign of relenting. Morris knew he was being studied.

Finally Percival answered:

"It is a public place; *anybody* can come here."

Morris understood then that more than a statement, this was a painful admission of the inevitable.

"I'll be off soon. I am only here on a brief visit. Besides, it is going to rain soon and I hate getting wet. What's your name?"

Carefully the boy examined the stranger once more, before entrusting him with something so important as his name.

Finally he spoke:

"I am called Percival. People always ask one's name because they think that names are of little importance. But to name something is to some extent to own it. I like my name. My mother gave it to me. Percival was a famous knight who belonged to the order of the Holy Grail. His deeds inspired a poet called Chretien de Troyes whom my mother deeply admires. I have been very lucky. With another mother I could be called John, Charles or Henry. Wagner also wrote a work about Percival. Are you an exhibitionist?"

Morris jumped and immediately glanced at his fly, a fact which did not go unnoticed by the boy; everything was in order.

"I'm asking you," explained Percival, "because the park is full of exhibitionists, rapists, murderers and that kind of person. They come to this lonely place to take advantage of the lack of police surveillance. I know some by sight, because at times they become regular visitors here. Then they disappear. That's why there are no girls in the park; their parents won't let them come. Fortunately I'm a boy."

"Don't worry," reassured Morris. "Up to now I have

not been an exhibitionist, not at least in the sense in which you use the word.''

"If you intend to remain here a while," Percival commented gravely, "it might be a good idea to come to an agreement about the use of language. It might start to rain any minute and we must establish who is in charge.''

"I am perfectly happy to accept *your* use of language," conceded Morris. "It's pretty and less arbitrary than many I know. It is even a little poetical.''

"It's because I am called Percival," the boy agreed with pleasure. "My mother is a very intelligent woman. *Intelligent and sensuous*," he repeated. "She would never use a word that did not sound well. That's why she lives alone. That is, she lives with me. Men, the rest of men, would never understand her. They lack sensuousness. If you are not an exhibitionist, are you a writer?''

Morris looked at the darkening sky. A whiff of wet honeysuckle reached him.

"More or less," he answered. "In fact," he said so as not to disappoint the boy, "I do write a little, though I don't think as well as Chretien de Troyes.''

"Do you smell the honeysuckle?" asked Percival. "I have been looking for it for some time, but I can't find it. It must be hidden behind some other bush. Although one could be confused. There is also a smell of wisteria coming from the west. By the lake they seem to blend.''

He lifted his small nose, sniffing the air like a trained dog, without any sign of self-consciousness. "I adore smells. I have inherited my mother's sense of smell, which is very sharp. Unfortunately the world is full of bad odours. That's why I come to the park every day. To disintoxicate myself. It is not surprising that you are not as good as Chretien de Troyes. It was a different world then, so my mother says. People had the vocation of becoming saints then. And now we have lost it and nothing replaces it. The world is full of hooligans who come to the park to throw rubbish into the lake."

A few drops had begun to fall and Percival stretched out his open hands. Morris noticed that they were white with fine long fingers.

"But there is no solution," continued Percival, and Morris wondered whether he was referring to the rubbish in the lake or to the loss of saintly vocations. "Do you like smells? Have you noticed the smell of the wet bark of trees? My mother took me once to an exhibition of 'olfactory sensations'. It was fantastic. At first I feared I might not go because I had a cold. I got chilled by the rain when I had the idea of undressing in it one day. But fortunately the cold proved no obstacle. I smelt more smells than in all my life. All kinds of smells. I came out feeling excited as if I had been drinking. Do you get drunk often?"

"Not often," answered Morris. "I prefer to read."

"So does my mother," said Percival. "Do you know the Saga of the Nibelungs? My mother can read German, French, and English. She is now learning Spanish in order to read Cervantes. Gosh! Look at that lightning!"

It was raining softly, just enough to make the leaves quiver and to darken the earth. The dome protected them but there were holes in the roof and water began to drip slowly, forming little lakes in the pitted floor.

"Soon you will hear the frogs croaking," Percival said knowingly. "Nobody imagines that there are frogs hiding in the reeds by the lake. But there are. They croak only when it rains. I don't know what they do the rest of the time. The life of animals is mysterious. Don't you think so?"

"So is the life of some people," answered Morris ambiguously. "What does your mother do?"

"She loves me," was Percival's surprising answer; he sounded completely natural. He was looking down at a small puddle forming on the edge of the bandstand.

"I think we all love you," agreed Morris.

Percival did not answer; he either agreed or thought the statement had no importance.

"Not long ago," continued Morris, "I read in the paper that in Moscow it rained frogs and toads. I would have liked to see it. The frogs and toads had been sucked up into an enormous cloud in the upper regions of the atmosphere, along with vapour condensation. Afterwards, as electrical charges precipitated the water, the frogs and the toads came down together with the rain. People got quite scared; they thought that the end of the world had come."

Percival was looking at him with curiosity, attentively following his words. It was still raining and more lightning appeared in the distant sky.

"Careful," Morris said, "you are getting wet."

"Are you sure of what you've told me?" asked the boy suspiciously. "People seem to think that to spin a string of nonsense is good for one. They call it *fantasy*"—he added with contempt—"while what is really marvellous is life itself; it's enough to look at it. Only idiots spend their time inventing things in order to appear imaginative, and they miss the fantastic in everyday life."

"I wouldn't lie to you for anything in the world," said Morris.

"It's all right. You look like an honest man, without that kind of fantasy I was talking about."

The sky had become darker; papers and leaves were

145

flying in the wind, seeds were hauled about in the air and the broken glass rattled.

Morris took his jacket off and covered the boy. Percival's fine hair was wet. And so were his shoes; they were white plimsoles, but there were several holes in them. Inside the man's navy jacket Percival looked very small and Morris felt a great desire to hug him. Whenever wet strands of his ash-coloured hair stuck to his face, the child made an impatient gesture to remove them because their wetness irritated him.

"As soon as it stops," Morris announced, "I would like to take you home, if you don't mind."

The boy, who had been silent for a while, looked at him suddenly with a certain sadness.

"No, thank you," he said. "I shall go back to the ducks."

Morris realized that he had been interfering and became uneasy; he felt a sense of guilt.

"It's almost dark," he added timidly, "and the ducks will have gone to sleep. I shall go and you have the stand all to yourself. It is really a beautiful stand, worthy of a Percival, knight of the Holy Grail, inspirer of Wagner and Chretien de Troyes."

"A duck died suddenly the other day," said Percival, wrapped in the navy jacket and becoming more melancholy by the minute. The unstable moods of poets and children, thought Morris.

"*Died suddenly*, do you understand, Mo?"

Morris was dismayed; the boy was not only moody, but now unexpectedly familiar and inventing a nickname.

"They had poisoned it," continued Percival, "they gave it poisoned food. I saw it, stretched on the ground, whiter than ever. Its feathers were swaying in the wind;

146

but the duck was still. Was dead. It looked so innocent... Do you know what I mean? They had taken advantage of its innocence. Somebody had thrown a bit of bread and the duck had behaved as expected. It is expected that ducks eat morsels of bread and any small thing they find in the water without asking anything from anybody. How was it to know? Apparently it suffered. I know because the park-keeper told me. He told me that it had suffered a lot and that it had taken a long time to die. He was sad also, because he loves his ducks. Who could feel angry with a duck? And that was not the only time. There have been other cases, but on such occasions the park-keeper noticed that the bread had a strange colour and fished out all the bits before the ducks got to them."

Percival was shivering under the navy jacket and Morris realized that it had become quite cold and dark and that the boy was determined not to go away. All the same he tried:

"Percival," he said, "it's late. I'm going to take you home; if you like, we can have a hot drink before. Your hair is wet, your feet are wet, and most likely your mother is worrying about you. When you have a mother who is so intelligent and so sensuous as to give you such a name, you must not upset her; it would not be a kind thing to do."

"No," insisted the boy. "I've told her that we had a football match at school and that I would be late. I am going to stay here with the ducks. They are all alone, nobody takes care of them at night. They don't bother anybody, they just live, just live. Until an idiot comes to the lakeshore with bits of poisoned bread, and when nobody is looking throws them into the water. And the ducks eat them because nobody has told them not to. It's normal and they have been doing it since the beginning of things; they eat because they have to eat and don't understand why a *natural* act must all of sudden be subverted. Yes, subverted. I know the meaning of this word."

Morris knew that he was in the presence of a knight of the Holy Grail, that there was no way of dissuading him from his noble decision, that his was a saintly vocation which brought back a past now forgotten, but from which at times still streamed sparks of light.

"I write to be read not to be heard," admitted Morris. "So be it; it looks as if your ducks are good people and worthy of your protection. If you'll allow me, I'll keep vigil with you: four eyes see more than two; besides a knight never refused the help of another, when fighting for a noble cause. Please give me permission to stay."

Percival, still shivering, managed a smile and snuggled near Morris, allowing him to rub his back to warm him up. "You don't have to worry about the dark," he said to Morris, "I keep a flashlight in the hollow of a tree trunk. It gives a very good light and one can see the ducks easily in the dark because they are white."

"I have full confidence in all the arrangements you have made," answered Morris. "You are an intelligent boy and I'm sure you have planned it all to perfection."

"I inherited my mother's intelligence," Percival confided, once again in a positive mood. "She got married young, but soon divorced. What my father wanted was a cook and a mistress by his side; not a companion. They quarrelled a lot on account of this, until they separated. I think that deep down Lancelot loved Percival."

"It's possible," agreed Morris, "but what does your mother think?"

"Oh, she has rather conventional views of things," answered Percival. "But the day she reaches a more mature attitude, I will discuss it with her."

The rain had stopped; isolated drops were still falling from the roof and landing heavily on the ground.

"I would also like you to be a knight of the Holy Grail," said Percival to Morris as they were leaving the stand.

Morris took him by the hand, lifted him in his arms and very gently kissed him on the mouth.

Then they went to look after the ducks.

Next week Morris wrote from the city the following letter to Ecks:

Dear old friend,

I have not been caught in the intricate bureaucratic nets of the Great Navel, as could have easily happened. Nor have I been run over by a native madman in his car, because I have gone out very little. All the same I am not planning to return home for the present. It is difficult to explain my change of plans. To avert your anxiety and possible lack of sleep, and also to pre-empt any supposition, hypothesis, deduction, and investigation (there is a lot of rumbling going on in the navel), I will tell you the reason without further ado: I have fallen madly in love with a nine-year-old boy. His name is Percival. His mother is delightful, *intelligent and sensuous*, to use her son's words. Together we three—a magic number full of cabbalistic references—form a rather eccentric group, as you may imagine. Percival is beautiful, loving and wise. I wish you could meet him. I admire his way of living.

At present we are still in the city; soon we shall leave for Africa. Percival wants to see the giraffes close up. He feels great affection for them, and I think the exoticism of that continent will fascinate him. He has never seen

150

anything outside Europe. I shall be working for a scientific expedition as a specialist in Lepidoptera.

Percival's mother has happily agreed to come; she is a great woman, full of curiosity and enthusiasm. She plans to give language lessons. We should be off by the end of the month. I have only got the time to carry out the necessary arrangements; I shall not be able to come and say good-bye.

I should like to give Percival my telescope. Could you please send it? Thank you very much. Percival is insatiably curious.

Best regards,

Morris.

On the same day Morris sent Graciela another letter:

Dearest Graciela,

The immortal gods decide the destiny of men. This in few words means that I have fallen in love with an enchanting little boy of nine called Percival. I will spare you the relevant literary references. Percival possesses (never was the word better employed) a mother, who is an intelligent attractive and sensitive woman, with whom he has lived from the day of his birth. The father, who was a great hindrance, disappeared from the scene long ago. He renounced the inconvenience of an intelligent and educated wife for the discreet comforts of a woman who knows how to cook and pot the plants. To each his own.

The least that can be said of us three together is that we form a picturesque group. We shall go to Africa. I can't wait to see Percival in an environment which is so remote from the present one. We are looking for a school for him to attend; though he might not learn anything new, he does need a little discipline. He wouldn't like to hear me saying this. All the same I will read him this letter before I post it, because he is rather touchy. *Marvellously so.*

I will write again soon.

Till then,

Morris.

P.S. He has now read the letter and says he will send you a lovely drawing of a rabbit. He enjoys drawing and does it very well. By the way, I'd be grateful if you could send me the astronomer's chronograph I've left in the library. Percival would love it.

After receiving Morris's letter Ecks dismantled the telescope which was kept in the garden and dispatched it in a box with the accompanying note:

Dear Morris,

Hell is not being able to love.

Ecks

Two days after, Graciela found Morris's chronograph on a shelf in his library. She blew off the dust, placed it in a box and sent it to him with these words:

My dear Morris,

I hope that Percival enjoys the chronograph. I assume that it still works, though I haven't tried it. But you can best show him all its secrets.
Hell is not being able to love.

Graciela

The departure of Morris left a sense of emptiness in the house. Winter was approaching, and Graciela and Ecks began to make plans to leave the island. Graciela was writing an essay on the oppression of women from the nineteenth century to the Second World War, and she needed to go to the Great Navel to consult some sources. As for Ecks, caught up as usual in the problem of papers and permits, he needed to get his residency card and find a job.

So they closed the house and went to the city, leaving the island, not without regret. They would share the fortunes and misfortunes of their new lives like two good friends.

The section on the left between the circle which floats on the waters (the firmament) and the circle of fish and birds, is dedicated to the birth of Eve. As the tapestry is woven the first man, Adam, is holding at rib-level a female figure smaller than himself but distinctly similar in appearance. This legend accompanies the scene: Inmisit Dominus soporem in Adam et tulit unam de costi ejus *(God put Adam to sleep and took out one of his ribs). Here too are plants and flowers similar to the ones which surrounded Adam in his solitude; there is also a tree with the words* Lignum pomiferum, *which remind us of the Garden of Eden and of the Tree of Good and Evil.*

This section completes the circle around the Creator. Inside it is written: In Principio Creavit Deus Celum Et Terram Mare Et Omnia Quoe In Eis Sunt Vidit Deus Cuncta Que Fecerat Et Erant Valde Bona (*In the beginning God created the heavens, the earth, the sea and all the things which inhabit them and God saw that all the things which he had made were good*).

Thus the marvellous weaver completed his representation of the beginning of the world according to the Holy Scriptures.

In the four corners he also portrayed the months of the year and the different tasks to be carried out therein.

155

Eve

The tribal rites I have attended from birth are now second nature to me. Like all the initiated, I find myself unable to ignore the ceremonial words and images handed down through the centuries by our medicine men. Once submitted to the incantations, traditional games, dances and sacrifices, I cannot escape. The woman who does so is ostracized and dies alone or mad. One must stay inside the temple, the house of our relentless gods, and collaborate in perpetuating the myths which sustain the structure, ideology and spirit of the tribe. Any conflict arising from our forced condition must be hidden.

Whenever I feel a certain repugnance for the ritual gesture, I can go to the woods and cry, or cleanse myself of a morning in the river.

(Fragment from *Eve, Her Confessions*, unpublished).

It Takes Two to Get Born
But Only One is to Blame

FROM THE DAILIES

A judge from Dalry (Scotland) passed judgement yesterday against a young woman who had allowed herself to become pregnant despite knowing of and having access to contraceptives. Twenty-two-year-old Christine, mother of a girl of three, had filed suit against a former boy-friend of hers, as father of the child. The judge condemned the mechanic Robert McCurdie to pay nominal child support of £1.00 per week, while severely reprimanding Christine for her negligence. She defended herself by saying that her doctor had advised against use of the contraceptive pill.

Graciela asked forty school children between the ages of seven and twelve to describe Adam and Eve in Paradise. These were some of the answers she received:

Adam was living very happily among the trees and the flowers when Eve arrived and made him eat the apple because she wanted to kill him and reign alone.

God created Eve from one of Adam's ribs because he was bored and wanted somebody to order about.

Adam was perfectly happy playing with the fish and the plants until Eve come and begun to bother 'im. He then give 'er a coupla whacks and tells 'er to be'ave 'erself but they et the apple all the same.

He was alone and wasn't happy because he couldn't chat with anybody, but when Eve came things got even worse.

God created Adam and surrounded him with plants, birds and fish, but he needed a companion. So God put him to sleep and created Eve out of a rib from his chest. Adam was happy then. The problems started because she was a bit curious and began listening to the serpent. Because of Eve we women have got a bad reputation in this world.

It seems to me that Adam was not a bad fellow. He went hunting and fishing, and walked in the forest planting trees. But, of course, he had nobody to talk to... So God came and gave him some pills to make him sleep and took out one of his ribs which grew and was called Eve. Eve was a woman. Adam was a man. So what had to happen happened. And that's how we were born.

My dad says that Eve was like all women who spend their time gossiping with their neighbours and are always bothering men to buy them clothes and things.

Adam was a little bored because God had not given him any games or things to amuse himself. All he had were the fish and the plants. So God gave him Eve to play with. But they quarrelled.

The story is confusing because I can't understand why God had the idea of giving Eve to Adam as a companion. If instead of a woman he had given him a man, Adam would have been much happier. They would have gone fishing, hunted wild animals, and on Saturday night they would have gone to the pub together.

I think that the whole story of Paradise is a metaphor because what the Bible tells us does not sound at all credible. First of all I don't understand why God, who created man in his own likeness, made him so that he became lonely and bored. Next, the idea that he took a rib out of Adam seems far-fetched. Why would he use that method just once, when afterwards we have all been born from our mother's tummy? I think it is all a matter of symbols. But I am not sure what they are symbols of, since in our church they only teach us the New Testament, which is what matters to the priests because of the business of "You are Peter and on this stone I shall build my church".

As a second task Graciela asked the children to imagine the daily life of Adam and Eve. Here are some of the answers:

Adam went about hunting the animals, lions, tigers and sheep. Eve cleaned the house and did the shopping.

Adam was a brave fighter. He went out at night to frighten the lions while Eve who was a bit lazy went on sleeping. Then they ate what he had brought home and with the skins they made themselves clothes which was hard work because in those days they had no electric light nor sewing machines. It was all done by hand.

Eve looked after the house which was a wild cave. Adam went out fishing and came back late but she always waited for him so that they could have supper together and afterwards she washed up.

Each one did the jobs proper to their sex. Which were: the man hunted fished and lit the fire, explored the area and from time to time smoked a cigarette. She remained at home in Paradise, cleaning and sewing because they did not go around naked any more.

As my father says, Adam always did the heavier jobs because he was stronger, more handsome, and better with the bow and arrows. He also says Eve wasn't pretty at all, but it was overlooked because there was nobody to compare her with, but she took revenge and made him eat the apple, and then they both had tummy ache.

Since she had a lot of free time (all she had to do was to wait for him to come home, and clean and cook the fish) she started walking among the trees and the snakes, and that's when she started having bad thoughts.

Adam worked hard to keep the two of them alive growing potatoes salad tomatoes and rice, and from time to time he brought home a deer or a lion to eat while lazy old Eve was doing nothing because she didn't have to go to the supermarket and besides she had no children.

And so Adam told her: If you want to acquire the knowledge of good and evil go on, I don't mind, but you must keep on cleaning the house and doing the ironing—that's your job.

Adam was very busy: not only he had to look after Paradise as God had told him to, but he also had to get the food. Besides I think he was in charge of public relations because it was he who talked directly to God and not Eve.

Adam was very serious and full of responsibilities and didn't know that while he was walking through God's countryside she had started chatting to the serpent who was very cunning and deceived her. It was all a woman's plot.

I think that after the story of the apple they weren't getting on so well but they couldn't separate because in those days there was no divorce and besides they had a new baby every year.

Concerning the virtues and faults of Adam and Eve, these are the statistical results obtained by Graciela:

Adam was brave (35); honest (23); hardworking (38); intelligent (38); responsible (29); obedient (22). His main fault was to listen to women (33).

Eva had only one virtue: being beautiful (30). One pupil said Eve was curious, but he wasn't sure whether this was a virtue or a defect.

On the other hand the list of Eve's faults was much longer: 39 pupils described her as excessively curious; 33, a gossip; and 25 thought that she had a bad temper. 22 said that she was lazy and 3, that she was frivolous.

After doing their work the children went out to play.

The circle in whose segments are represented the most important moments of the creation is located within a larger rectangle. In each of its corners a winged angel blows a horn from which the winds escape. With their legs the angels straddle like riders leather bags which also contain wind. The writing in the lower right corner says: Auster *(Southern). The figures of the angels are surrounded by small triangles filled with curving lines; this is the way the ancient weaver represented the lands and mountains over which the winds fly. Everything here indicates movement: the air escaping, the full leather bags, the studied position of the limbs of the angels as if they were riding. The inclusion of the winds, so close to the circle of Creation, at the side of the Creator Himself, suggests that all is moving; nothing in the Universe remains still.*

The Journey, XIX: London

What is amazing is that revelations are unclear.

Ecks

A question floated in the dream, an enigma, the sort of riddle that kings, in love with their daughters, use to fend off aspiring suitors.

Princes and knights go to the scaffold, tempted to solve the conundrum that keeps the daughters for their fathers alone.

In his dream Ecks heard this question:

"What is the greatest tribute and homage a man can give to the woman he loves?"

Ecks has found work with a transport company: he is in charge of a service which takes pregnant women to London for abortions. He does not have to drive, because there is already a driver; he has to accompany the passengers to their destination, leave them at the clinic, collect them after the operation and take them back to the city. He does this once a week. Though he is not too happy with his new job, he knows that there is not much choice at present.

"Look at it this way," the fat man who manages the company tells him, "there's no risk of being made redundant in this line of work. It's the second oldest profession. And becoming more popular by the day..."

The fat man smokes a stinking cigar; this disturbs Ecks almost as much as his squinting eyes, one of which looks towards the city and the other towards London.

Each week the fat man gives Ecks a printed list of the names of the women he is to take care of. The demand is growing and at times the coach is not big enough.

The office where the women reserve their places for the journey is situated in the centre of the city; a large building, but neglected and dirty. There are no chairs and the women have to stand in line for their turn. Behind the counter, on which are placed two dried up ink-pots, sits fat José and a clerk whose job it is to give the women information about the round trip to the London clinic. The room has no natural light; it is lit by two sad white neon strips fixed onto the wall.

Anxious and tense, the women queue in front of the office door long before José (sweaty, cigar in mouth) appears, exuding paternalism and false protectiveness.

"Ladies, please!" he shouts, taking out the key, as the women surround him. (A poor sultan in a mediocre harem, thinks Ecks in silence.) "Don't push! Don't get so excited! There's a place for everyone. Wait your turn. Soon you will be in London and able to rid yourselves of your small bundles."

José enjoys and laughs at his own jokes: "See how these girls love travelling?" he says winking at Ecks who stands silent and docile at his side. "Don't knock each other down! There is room for everyone! And if there isn't at present," continues José, pleased with his own wit, "you can go a while later, yes? Can't you wait a few weeks? Why not?" José laughs loudly. He looks at Ecks and says: "They are like children. Now they're crying because I have said that they have to wait a few weeks. Okay, ladies, I was joking. We shall do all we can to get you all out this week and those who can't go now will go on the next coach. And your husbands will be very happy."

The office smells, but nobody minds. The women crowd around the counter to receive the forms they have to fill in.

"Remember," shouts the fat man, "no lies. If you are more than three months pregnant by the time you get to London, nothing doing. No butcher will deal with you. The company is not responsible under the circumstances and does not return the money. So, no lies. You for instance, dear lady, your tummy looks already a considerable size. What?'' he laughs, ''only two months? Go and tell the marines... You'd better have your baby. It is not my fault! I am not the man you went to bed with...''

The coach trip is silent and sad. The women are not in a talkative mood; they prefer either to sleep or to pretend to sleep. Ecks does not try to cheer them up; he hardly dares to look at them: a sense of shame prevents him. At times he would like to sink into his seat alongside the driver and simply disappear, wiping out his share of responsibility in the whole event.

Occasionally, but not often, one of the women, unable to sleep, gets up from her seat and goes to him under the pretext of having run out of cigarettes. Ecks always brings along a whole carton on the journey, but then he hesitates: it seems to him that to offer cigarettes all around would be offensive. The women—accidentally and briefly thrown together in this ghetto-like situation— would feel even more the affront to their identity. He also senses that sharing anything, however inconsequential and incidental, that belongs to this humiliating experience makes them hostile towards each other. The fact of being pregnant is in this way like being born with the wrong skin colour, coming from the wrong side of the tracks, being an exile or amputee: nobody has sympathy to spare for fellow sufferers.

The long journey holds little attraction. Ecks feeds the travellers with soft music, hoping that the almost identical tunes will create a state of hypnosis, inducing relaxation. But an anxious mind does not quiet easily.

Even during the two short spells when the driver stops to eat and drink there is very little contact among the women. They drink mineral water, leave their meals almost untouched and chain-smoke. So does Ecks. Seated at the table where the driver eats with good appetite, he silently rejects the man's coarse comments on the passengers, aimed at creating a kind of comradery between the two of them. Instead, he attempts to do the crosswords in the newspapers; he always travels with a large quantity of them and of magazines, for the benefit of the women in the coach.

Once a week Ecks arrives at the clinic with his load of bulging women. All is prepared for a quick and efficient intervention. One by one, with the same helpless look, the women enter the many operating rooms while Ecks crosses their names from the list. Smoking a cigarette, the receptionist enquires about the city's football teams; sometime he asks Ecks to make a bet on the pools or to bring him back a pornographic magazine. Inevitably, as each of the travellers comes out of her operating room, the receptionist goes up to her with a smile full of false concern and pats her encouragingly on the back:

"It went very well, madam; you look fine. Hope to see you again soon."

The clinic has its touches; this receptionist, for instance, is an immigrant who speaks the same language as those who come for abortions.

"I have a good eye," he tells Ecks. "I've seen thousands of women come through here, yet I am still able to pick out faces . I know some who've already been here a couple of times. I greet them with special attention, they're good customers. They all swear: 'never again' but sooner or later they come back. It's life. Some even come back within two months. Would you believe it?"

The girl came late when all the seats had been sold. José had completed the list and handed it to Ecks who automatically checked it from top to bottom to make sure that no name appeared twice or had been omitted. The fat man was breathing noisily because of the heat, puffing away at his eternal smelly cigar. The girl had short, blond hair which hardly reached her cheek bones; her complexion was white as a baby's, and her blue eyes were deep and penetrating. The colour of her dress almost matched their intensity.

"Please," she told José. "It's imperative that I go this week. I'm already in the third month..."

José grabbed the medical certificate from her hand.

Ecks was leaning against the wall, smoking: the heat was unbearable and he was longing to turn off the neon bulbs whose milky light reminded him of the clinic in London, of ugly hospitals where old people died alone without money or memories, of barred cells in a zoo.

The fat man returned the certificate to the girl without ceremony.

"Three months and twenty five days," he said severely. "Nothing doing. Besides, there are no seats left in tomorrow's coach, nor in the next one; we are full for the next two weeks. Why didn't you do something

171

about it before?"

He turned his head in the direction of Ecks, seeking both his complicity and an audience for the usual theatrical pronouncements: "Plenty of speed when it comes to jumping into bed, but afterwards...I can't take you. We give no priorities. And as you may imagine, in this kind of journey no passenger wants to give up her place. What have you been doing during the last four months? You weren't thinking of having the kid, were you?"

Ecks felt oppressed by the light: did he need glasses?

"I was looking for the money," explained the girl softly. "It hasn't been easy; I'm unemployed."

"I've heard this story before, young lady," answered José bluntly. "This is the way the business is run. Did you expect to pay in installments?"

"Please," entreated the girl.

José was becoming cross.

"Utterly impossible," he said. "Off you go. Come back next time with longer notice. Next year with the next pregnancy."

(A German pharmaceutical company on several occasions requested the Nazi authorities to dispatch three or four hundred pregnant Jewesses for experimental purposes. It was a good way of reducing numbers in the camps.

"*We gratefully acknowledge receipt of your latest cargo,*" wrote the company director in 1938. "*We have carried out tests with a new chemical substance. No survivors. However, around the end of October we are planning a new series of experiments, for which we shall require another three hundred subjects. Could they be provided on the same conditions as previously?*")

172

The blue eyes had clouded over.

Ecks threw down his cigarette-butt and crushed it underfoot.

It was too hot. Outside and inside.

Ecks overtook her before she reached the corner. She looked startled as she turned towards him.

"Excuse me," he said nervously. "There may be a way. I may be able to take you, if you'll occupy my seat by the driver. I can stand up or sit in the alleyway on top of my suitcase. Once in London, we'll be able to find another clinic. The service will be the same and so will the cost. I don't think the driver will mind. It has never happened before; he can just pocket the price of your ticket."

There was no answer: she looked down, her dress only a little paler than her eyes.

"The coach leaves tomorrow," continued Ecks softly.

"I have nowhere to stay," she confessed without emotion. "If they find out at the agency, will you lose your job?"

"I don't think so," Ecks lied. "I will pick you up somewhere on the way. No one else checks the list once we have left. I have a room near here. If you want to, you can stay there. It's not very big, but there's an old sofa."

"Thanks," she said simply.

(A month after receiving his shipment, the pharmaceutical director had written again to the German authorities:

"*The women you sent this time were very thin and weak. The majority had infectious diseases. Nevertheless*

173

we managed to use all of them—no survivors. We await your next dispatch in two weeks' time. With thanks and best regards.")

When Graciela came home, Ecks was reading the paper and the girl was sleeping lightly on the sofa. Without making a sound, Graciela went to the little cooking area, hidden in a cupboard. Ecks followed her and explained what was happening. Graciela made some tea in silence, anxious not to disturb the girl. She had no other luggage apart from her bag which hung from the back of the sofa.

They drank their tea without a word; Graciela showed Ecks a letter from Morris which had arrived that morning. It was addressed to both of them and related some episodes of his stay in Africa. But mainly it talked of Percival and his mother Eve. There was a special section for Graciela in which Morris wrote about the practices of cliterodectomy and infibulation effected on young girls in various countries; he also marked the areas that Graciela should visit to see for herself and offered to accompany her. Morris described how at the age of twelve—normally after the first menstrual period—the women (or children?—he asked) were taken away from their villages and led to secluded areas where their clitoris and labia were excised by means of knife, sharp stone or any other cutting object. The vagina was then sewn with coarse thread or thorns. This process practically sealed the girls' vulvas. The cuts would scar-over within a couple of weeks, if they did not turn septic and lead to death from infection, of which there were many instances. The survivors were then returned to their villages, where they were now considered ready to be sold as brides, concubines or auctioned at the clothes and fruit markets. Infibulation was repeated whenever a girl was to be resold, or whenever her owner decided. In certain communities, Morris explained, this practise had the character of a ritual, an offering to the gods. Whoever purchased a girl had the right to test the effectiveness of the infibulation before paying the price.

Graciela was choking on her tea, something she often did when she tried to eat too many biscuits with it.

"A delicate business," whispered Ecks mockingly. "Coach-loads of pregnant women, infibulated girls, and whales committing suicide on the Atlantic shores where they should know the fish are all poisoned."

"I think I'll go," said Graciela, playing with the edge of her paper napkin.

"Let us infibulate," continued Ecks with his tendency to repeat the things that disgusted him, either to exorcise or accustom himself to them.

"It was kind of Morris to invite you," he added in a tone of voice which Graciela was unable to interpret. "But why didn't he invite me? I could leave my job as an abortion guide and become the official infibulator in some African kingdom. I would insert the thorns with extreme delicacy and even paint them bright colours to incite fresh buyers.

"If you go, don't forget your great-grandmother's chastity belt, the charming iron one with spikes. And mind you close it well with two turns of the key. Doña Zacarías would be very happy in her tomb, knowing that her favourite belt was coming to the aid of her great-granddaughter."

When the girl woke up—she said her name was Lucía—they offered her tea and biscuits. Ecks played some music and then went to bed because the journey

175

the following day promised to be uncomfortable as well as long. But he was unable to sleep. Whenever he shut his eyes he saw huge thorns or soldiers in uniform.

They picked up Lucía in a side street before leaving the more crowded areas of the city. The coach stopped briefly and she jumped in. No word was spoken. The other women, wrapped up in their thoughts, wore that helpless and at once resentful look which normally put Ecks off from even offering them a drink of water or a cigarette. Lucía handed the driver a number of bank notes which he scrupulously counted and put away in a little bag inside his shirt. Then he revved the engine and they were off. Ecks gave Lucía his seat and stood up for a while looking out the window. Not much to look at: the streets were all alike, monotonous grey blocks where workers from the nearby factories lived. Lines of freshly-washed laundry hung from the small balconies; the flowerpots were of the same reddish colour as the dried-up soil.

"I haven't been to a London theatre yet," Ecks suddenly said to Lucía. He felt he could talk to her; it was the first time that he had a real desire to talk to anybody during these journeys.

She looked at him attentively.

"The-a-tre," repeated Ecks as if talking to a foreigner. "Do you understand what I mean?" (He addressed himself to her using the polite form as he always did with women he was not acquainted with; a linguistic habit derived from the many nineteenth-century novels he had read, and one which he was unable to break.)

She nodded affirmatively. But Ecks was not convinced.

"A theatre," he explained, "where things are

represented—as in real life," he added, "with the only difference that one is sitting facing the action—if not looking down on it from higher up in the circle. I often have nightmares about the theatre: I sit in my seat but instead of looking at the stage, I present my back to it, or my side; and I am the only one in that position. Embarrassing, don't you think? In vain I try to turn my seat in line with the rest, in order to face the stage; as soon as I succeed, the stage inexplicably moves once again behind my back and I am still missing the spectacle. Very unfortunate. At other times I buy my ticket like everybody else and go up the stairs to get to my seat in the circle but I can't find the entry; curtains surround me, confuse me; I go up and down endless lines of stairs and never reach the right place. Even worse, at times I find myself in the middle of the stage, like one of the actors, without knowing my part. They are dreams full of anxiety and I call them my theatrical dreams. I imagine that, if the theatre is a representation of life, theatrical nightmares are images of images, twice removed from reality. I sometimes dream that I am acting and in my role I am often asleep."

"I always dream that I am a child," Lucía said. "It looks as if I am unable to grow up. I *am* a child even if I don't look it. If we are still ourselves in our dreams, I wonder from what angle we see ourselves, our clothes, our appearance? Often in the very dreams I am disturbed by this thought. I think I wake up and I go on looking at myself as if I were myself and somebody else at the same time; and afterwards I am not sure whether I was awake then, or still dreaming. It is all so unclear."

"Few words are spoken in dreams," went on Ecks. "In this, dreams differ fundamentally from theatre; if we were deaf in our dreams, very little would change."

"I don't like the theatre," said Lucía. "They speak far too fast for me; my ears can't follow them. At times I would like to stop the performance, to *crystallize* it, as one fixes an image in time and space, and be able to hear the words again and analyze them one by one. But I can't pause and think at every stage of the performance; before I have fully understood all the dimensions and levels of one sentence, they have pronounced another one. I must be stupid."

"A journey," said Ecks, "the theatre is like a journey without motion. I travel worlds, without ever leaving my seat."

"Dreams," said Lucía. "In them no one grows old, there is no progress. Scenes are repeated from dream to dream, with only small changes."

Ecks looked along the seats of the coach. Many women had fallen asleep, weighed down by their loneliness and their anxiety.

"What a strange load we carry," he thought aloud. "There are no innocent passages. My mother should have named me Charon."

"A tiny hole in the condom, and the London theatre beckons," was Lucía's melancholy answer.

"Professional habit," Ecks confessed; "when I walk through the streets, I often think of the number of petty accidents that gave birth to these crowds. An absurd and meaningless activity, I admit. Plane and coach-loads heading for London, truck-loads of female internees to the Nazis' pharmaceutical factories, unexpected conceptions in apparently cloistered wombs, disappearances on a mass scale, the twists of fate in a condom. An endless performance during which we appear on stage at inappropriate moments in front of an unseen public. Still, we improvise the script, and this is at once the incentive for and the source of our anguish. Thousands of condoms every day and one drop escapes and oils the chain of chance; if we break it, it is with the tormented awareness of having interfered, of transgressing arcane laws. It's like breaking with the ritual of prayers and entreaties which we offer up in return for favours from some divinity. *This is the chain of fortune. It has reached you now. If you follow these instructions within the stated time, all your wishes will come true; you will have good health, wealth and will be lucky in love. But you must not break the chain. Jane did and she had a heart attack. Peter forgot to complete the task and lost his job; Tony broke his arm. But John, who sent out all the letters in the time prescribed, won the pools! All you must do is make seven copies of this letter and send them to seven friends within three days from the date of receiving your copy. Also send a cheque for ten dollars to the name and address of the person at the top of the list. Don't forget to include your details at the bottom of the list and in a few weeks' time you will receive many such ten-dollar cheques. If you don't wish to take part in this, just send out the copies of the letter without sending money. At all costs, don't break the chain, or serious harm will come to you.* The chain of the condom, the chain of destiny.''

The coach travelled an iron bridge over an ancient river which was almost dry now; past a war memorial (the white stones of a cemetery could be glimpsed behind it) and a fountain that spouted coloured water.

"I am a sedentary man by nature," said Ecks. "All the same I have been obliged to travel almost all my life; in fact journeys are second nature to me. As the poet said, cities are a state of mind."

"I have never been outside the city," answered Lucía. "This is my first journey and I'm a little scared. Girls don't travel much, do they?"

"If we had time, I'd like to show you something of the streets of London and the old pubs. Lace curtains in windows. Symmetrical museums where time stands still. In these museums chance—or the condom, shall we say—is shut out. Or rather, chance is fixed in the time and space represented by the paintings on the walls. No longer chance, but cause and effect: the best way to handle chance, if only you succeed in catching it. But I doubt we will have any spare time. The length of our visit is calculated to the last minute, just enough to go in and out of the clinic. Plus a few hours rest in the hotel, but then I must stay in to check that nobody escapes. I am the invigilator, the mysterious guardian. But I'll be back another time."

"Not me. Never again will I let destiny slip by me in a drop, if there's anything I can do about it. The humiliation is not so much this bus, the silent journey, the clinic with its assembly-line service. The real humiliation is to know that you are the victim of chance, one more form of oppression. I'll never sleep with a man again. It's through them that fate enters our lives, subjugates us, poisons our beings. Never, never again. Men bring about our slavery, forge the chains. Never again."

Ecks was silent. They were now entering a part of the city without trees. Like men without phalluses, he thought.

The return journey was made at night and in silence. The driver preferred to travel without lights inside the coach, and most of the women slept. Sitting on his suitcase, Ecks felt choked by a sense of guilt and anger. Lucía, elbows on her lap, her blond head resting on clenched fists, was looking down at her shoes; she had refused to wear the cozy slippers which the clinic gave as presents to its clients.

Field hospitals for the war-wounded. Military hospitals housing political prisoners. Woods where troublesome opponents disappeared. Ships of fools, the ship as substitute for the madhouse. Evil-smelling prisons to lock up transgressors. Private clinics.

"Would you like a drink of water?" Ecks asked Lucía. His voice faltered.

She looked up with her doe-like blue eyes and shook her head. Ecks felt unbearably sure he would never forget that look glimpsed in the dark coach by the light of the shining dashboard. There are such memories which have no apparent importance; scenes that become fixed in the mind without one's intention to retain them. As if in a dream, Ecks looked at her, saw himself looking at her and, from afar, saw them both.

When they got off the coach, Lucía declined his offer of company. She gave him her hand, a soft blond hand, thanked him for his help and promised to come and visit him sometime. But never, never again. Gloomily Ecks watched her go. We know nothing about those we love, except our need for their presence.*

---

* "Between us there was a perfect match," thought Ecks later. "I loved her for reasons which had only to do with me, and she did not love me for reasons which had only to do with herself."

He entered a bar; no woman was to be seen there. What did women do when they were sad? Where did they go? Where did they take their melancholy? There weren't many public places for women; no doubt their bad moments were spent in loneliness among household objects, by the washing machine. Who had ever seen a woman of his age, of similar appearance—that is of indefinite appearance—walk in under the purple lights of a small bad-smelling bar, lean on the formica counter and just ask for a beer, and be served normally without arousing curiosity or suspicion, without an intruder approaching her, to ask her something with his fat smooth voice, and interrupt her silence? Only old women came, women addicted to drink, or "women of the world". Ecks almost shivered when he pronounced these last words: a strangely ambiguous expression which perhaps contained a hidden homage behind its contemptuous tone. To be a "woman of the world" meant to be nobody's woman, not the woman of Ecks, nor of the kitchen, nor of the children. It meant to belong to life, to which we all—that is all men—belong.

What did women do when they were sad? There are codes and rituals in most cases. A sad man enters a bar, asks for a beer, watches the silver bead running inside the pinball machines, looks sideways at his profile in the mirror, pretending to know this stranger, the guest of his own image; he possibly ends the night with some "woman of the world" ejaculating his semen in her arse, because that's why he has a penis and has money to pay for his pleasure. Where do women turn, in whose arse do they discharge their misery? Where could Lucía be now? Never again.

Extensions of stay are not allowed. This was part

of the instructions given to those on the coach to London. You go to a city in order to get into a clinic, come out, and go back. He couldn't really say that he had gone to London. This had begun to be a suspicious assertion. When a woman said in public, "Not long ago I went to London," all eyes would turn distrustfully towards her. That journey in the dark... And he had not had the time to invite her to the theatre, because extensions of stay are not allowed.

The Greeks used to stone them to death for adultery.

Ecks went back to his fusty, dark room. Graciela was tidying her things; she had finally decided to go to Africa to meet Morris and prepare a report on infibulation. She had got her camera ready, a pair of jeans, note-books, and not much else.

"The 'Jobs-Wanted' page decided me," she explained. "After three months all I have found to do is to sell cosmetics door-to-door. Some people have not yet realized that make-up is no longer in fashion. *Wanted: good-looking young lady with selling ability; salary based on percentage of sales*. As for the adverts which ask for chamber-maids, I have no desire to warm-up the beds of strangers. I could have done some strip-tease in the transvestite bars. It seems that I look quite attractive dressed-up as a man and with a bowler hat," she added, grabbing a broom and rehearsing a *tango*. "Some people go mad at the sight of a tie between two breasts. There is a letter for you from Percival with a lovely drawing of giraffes walking in the sun. I have pawned the radio, the electric fan, that blessed watch of my grandmother, the steam iron, Morris' spyglass and your marble *mah-jongg* set. I'm sorry. You'll be able to ransom it with your next pay cheque. Here is the ticket, don't lose it.

"The rest of the money for my ticket was sent by Morris. Apparently he found a very rare butterfly. I shall go by boat; it's cheaper and will give me the chance to study the coastal landscape. Why don't you come? Morris says it wouldn't be too difficult to find a place for everybody, that means for you too."

Ecks looked at her blankly:

"I think I'll stay this time," he murmured.

Graciela went up to him and kissed him on the forehead.

"There are journeys from which one doesn't return," she said tenderly.

The Journey, XX: A White Ship

Two days later Ecks accompanied Graciela to the boat; she had no luggage and had had her hair cut short as when he met her. It was a middle-sized ship, all white. This seemed a good omen to Ecks, who remembered an old superstition among sea-faring people about white ships. In the old days ships were never white for fear of being more easily spotted and captured by pirates or enemies. But the sailors of New England believed that white ships never sank because they were protected by the moon. The story goes that in the eighteenth century an old English sea-captain from Liverpool was caught with his entire fleet by a raging storm in the Molucca Sea, an area affected by southern monsoons. The captain ordered his crew to furl the mainsail, haul down the mizzen and tack. But the sail got torn and they had to bring down the spar. Then in the middle of the tempest, the captain had the rudder painted white. Suddenly, the wind abated and a full white moon appeared in the sky and accompanied the fleet during the rest of the crossing.

Ecks was pleased too that Graciela's trousers were white and her sandals also. "You will not travel alone," he told her, "the moon will go with you."

He gave Graciela a compass to remember him by, and an old silver coin which he had kept for a long time, for

Percival: his handsome drawing of giraffes deserved that sort of payment.

For several days Ecks tried to find Lucía wandering through the streets, sitting on a bench in the square, drinking a cup of coffee in a bar or visiting a museum. These were the kind of places he thought he would have liked—it would have been right—to find her. Yet he suspected that he was searching in vain. Only in imagination or dreams do the people we love occupy their proper places.

"It's difficult to trace somebody with so little information," the barman told him, handing him a beer. "You should have a photo, or at least know her surname." Personally, he thought you could find that sort of girl everywhere. Why was Ecks so fixed on this particular one? Why didn't he settle with somebody else? What was special about her? Just a young girl like the others, neither ugly nor beautiful, lost in the slums of the city, hiding in some dark room of a little hotel, eating badly, hardly sleeping, out of a job; she would end up behind the counter of some dirty old café, if not worse. Still, each to his own taste. He liked race horses; they were all different—Red Rum, Nijinsky, Galloping Major, Midsummer Walk...though some people were so thick that they could hardly tell one from the other.

"Have you seen the papers?" the barman asked Ecks.

Ecks said he hadn't. At times he lost interest in the news and preferred to ignore it. Not to read the papers was a way of distancing himself from the world: a powerless yet dignified rebellion.

"Take a look at this!" The barman, in his shirtsleeves, smoking a black cigarette, handed him the paper with a patronizing gesture, the kind of gesture with which one helps a stranger—not to please, but equally without any intent of gain; not to display generosity, but superior knowledge.

"Careful not to smudge the racing tips."

The front page showed a photograph of an elderly man and an even older woman in an overcoat; between them, like the officiating priest at a ceremony, stood a machine full of keys and buttons. The headline above said: A COMPUTER WITH A HEART. And the inscription in smaller characters went:

Horst Chebus, a 49-year-old clerk from Dusseldorf, has been reunited with his mother after 35 years. They were separated at the end of War World II, and each believed that the other had long been dead. Having fed his office computer with all the data relating to his mother, Horst was finally rewarded with the surprising news that she was still alive. Moreover, the computer was able to provide him with her current address.

"I wouldn't like to have to wait so long," said Ecks, returning the tabloid across the countertop.

"Thirty years," commented the barman, spitting between his yellow teeth. "Only for a mother could you wait so long (or for a horse, maybe). Think of them now, exchanging news and talking over their different lives."

Ecks moved slightly to avoid the stern glance of his reflection in the mirror.

"You should find a detective," the barman went back to the previous topic. "That's what they do in films and novels."

It was early in the day, and the bar was almost empty. Ecks paid and went out.

187

The Journey, XXI: The Enigma

In the dream there was a question. It hung like an enigma, like one of those riddles which kings in love with their daughters used to set for all the suitors. Princes and knights lost their lives in the foolish attempt to answer the obscure question, which kept the daughters only for their fathers' hands and eyes. In the dream Ecks heard the question: *"What is the greatest tribute and homage a man can give to the woman he loves?"*

Ecks went into the cheap restaurant and bought a lunch special: soup, main course and dessert, with a small pitcher of mineral water. The place was crowded as usual. Damp patches appeared on the green-painted walls. Sausages floated in fat, with a fried egg on the side.

Sometimes the suitor got a second chance to solve the riddle. The cursed blade would not chop off his noble but unfortunate head until after a second answer. All the while, the princess was secretly loved by the king under cover of darkness, when he would mistakenly call her by the name of his queen, or perhaps a slave.

Neon tubes nailed to the white ceiling cast a sad light. The paper tablecloths were removed and replaced after every meal. There ate old men, chewing slowly with their gums, penniless students and prostitutes. *The city of his memories or of his dreams, the imagined city*, thought

Ecks. Was this the answer? In the dream he heard the question in the midst of his confusion. He felt the tyranny of the ritual enigma weighing him down; surely the next time the blade would sever his head.

There was only one empty place, by the side of a sad-looking woman who was eating slowly and in silence, looking fixedly at the glass in front of her. Ecks joined her, carrying his plate along the narrow passage. The neon light was oppressive.

"May I sit here?" he asked the woman, pushing the chair back.

She looked at him in surprise. Someone had beaten her up the night before and her face was swollen. One eye, puffed, was watering; the other, deformed by blows, seemed to overflow along the cheek. (What is the greatest tribute a man can give to the woman he loves? Ecks was mentally repeating.)

Ecks sat down. Immediately the woman lowered her gaze, poor broken doll with pulled-out eyes. She was chewing with some difficulty, her jaw possibly dislocated by the beating. The bread proved too tough for her condition and she had to give up on it. Her movements were delicate and unobtrusive, as if she was determined to deny the existence of the black marks on cheeks and neck. Her white hands were wrinkled, with swollen veins; cheap, showy rings shone on her fingers: big green stones, chunks of glass, but the oxidized metal had stained the skin. She wore coarse bracelets on her thin wrists as an abandoned mongrel wears a worn-out collar. Yet the hands moved with a certain dignity.

Ecks saw that her glass was empty and poured her some water, though he did not know whether she was thirsty. Her left eye went on dripping intermittent tears

189

over the plate. All the same, seeing the full glass, she lifted her head and drank a sip of water. Just one. How strange, thought Ecks. Large bruises, blue shadows lengthening those on her face, could be seen down her neckline, with its absurd decolletage revealing dry, meatless breasts. The blouse was old, wrinkled, with holes where sequins once had sparkled. *You appear, burning all/With light and colour*, Ecks silently recited. She wore tight-fitting trousers in violet satin, black spike heels, very worn and twisted, on which only well-trained feet could find their balance.

The main course was potatoes and beans. The woman ate without interest, pricking the beans one by one with her fork; perhaps because she had problems chewing with her dislocated jaw. Though he had begun his meal later, Ecks was already well ahead of her.

"They don't allow dogs in," she said suddenly, without seeming to address him specifically. "In this place, I mean," she qualified. Ecks did not think this place would provide many left-overs for dogs; those who came to eat were all endowed with good appetites.

"They don't allow cats either," he muttered in compensation.

"Yesterday's lunch was a bit cold and did not agree with me," the woman went on. "What about you?"

"I didn't come yesterday," answered Ecks. "I slept."

The woman's eye went on watering but she seemed unaware of it. The blue swelling on her forehead was like a sad ornament that had slipped down from her hair.

"Spaghetti bolognese," she told Ecks. "It was cold, or maybe I came too late. We're having custard for dessert today."

"I could eat two," Ecks took up the conversation.

"They won't let you have two," she answered resentfully. The bracelets shook—a distant music, like the sound of empty cans rattling around an open space. Had she tried to fix her eyes on him, she wouldn't have been able to do so. They seemed to have overflowed out of their sockets, to have drowned under blows.

Ecks got up and brought back the two small dishes with the custard, without the woman ever looking at him. From a distance her bruises were just as conspicuous, but lost detail. The engorged veins on her forehead looked like a single blot; but up close they formed a little map with rivers and tributaries.

Ecks placed the dish before her. The flan quivered. Ecks gripped his spoon, but his hand hesitated before breaking the gelatinous surface.

"Seems well-chilled," he said encouragingly.

Beheaded suitors. Old kings in love with their daughters, inventing impossible puzzles. In the dark delirium of night confounding the names of the queen or the slave.

The woman was not prepared to let him go. Without either of them taking the initiative, they descended the stairs together, as if by accident. All the same she did not appear too sure of herself, partly because her self-confidence was low, partly because her intuition as a "woman of the world" had taught her to distrust her chances of success with men like him.

"Will you come with me?" she suggested without showing desire or enthusiasm, as if her proposal were not very tempting, like the jockey who starts after the race has begun, just to fulfill a contract. "My room is near here," she added for duty's sake.

In the dream the enigma went: "What is the greatest

tribute and homage a man can give...?"

Ecks shook his head.

She did not look so disappointed.

"It wouldn't cost you much," she added without emotion.

The clouds were low and perhaps that was why everything seemed grey.

Ecks repeated his gesture.

She then stroked his arm, lightly, only enough to make him look at her. That eye, the faltering spring, was still dripping.

"I'm having a few problems," she explained; her voice was hesitant. "All that matters is for us to be seen together...," she was beaten and did not mind begging, "...going up to my room..." She let the sentence go in the air, the way a wounded soldier lets go his shield.

Ecks followed her without speaking. Grey dirty pigeons were hoping in front of them. One limped, its right leg broken. They flew off, staying close to the ground, lacking imagination, perspective, the unsought horizon always out of reach.

At the foot of the stairway a sickly man sporting a page of greasy newspaper on his chest was begging for money; he flaunted his sores, only slightly larger than those the woman bore. Children with scabbed bare feet skipped through the cigarette-ends and orange peels. The air smelled of urine, damp laundry and fish soup.

They went up the stairs. The steps were high; some treads were missing. At one stage as he climbed Ecks experienced a moment of vertigo and his heart jumped with terror; he felt as if he had leapt into the void. He remembered the exiles' stories: simulated executions; hooded figures pushed towards the cliff's edge. But he

192

soon recovered; the stairs went on, dirty and smelly as before. He placed one foot before the other, carefully studying his movements. Sometimes he had experienced the same sensation when descending, that the stair stopped and that the step which he had just naively taken was throwing him into space. What most frightened him was not falling, but the awareness of the false step; that that chain of certitudes, whose sequence he had confidently trusted, suddenly gave way. "All the same we all have to die," Esks told himself.

When they arrived she pushed the door open.

They went in. Ecks saw a bed, a peeling mirror, a towel, a wash-bowl, a sink with an old tap, the framed photo of a well-known actor, an image of Christ, a jug with stiff plastic flowers. There was a window with the curtains closed, dirty and dusty. Clothes were piled up on the sofa. The radio, a dark oval-shaped cabinet, ancient and enormous, sat over a white hand-embroidered tablecloth. This radio was the only object which could be said to decorate the room; it showed that the owner was particularly fond of it, nurtured an uncontrollable passion for it, so to speak, as though it were a dog, a bird, or an unfinished game of patience.

She began to undress without being asked. She did it mechanically, without any attempt to act out happiness or pleasure.

Old kings—thought Ecks—in love with their daughters, set complicated enigmas, impossible riddles for ambitious suitors soon to lose their heads. What was the answer? The only correct answer which could stop the sacrifice?

The woman's body was battered; the scars looked as if painted with bright red sealing wax. Besides she had large varicose veins. Yet despite it all she had dignity. Her bones were slender, her limbs fleshless. She reclined on the bed with her head leaning on the board behind it. She made a gesture asking for a cigarette. Ecks offered it to her already lit. Her request was helping him, it brought him out of that silent passivity to which he had succumbed. It gave him back the use of his tongue and the freedom of his limbs.

"Good cigarette," the woman said to start the conversation.

He handed her the pack.

"I didn't ask for it. I don't want it," she protested.

Ecks thought that at times it is better not to give. Could that be the answer? he asked himself. "Do not give."

He put the pack back in his pocket.

"Aren't you going to take your clothes off?" she finally asked with some apprehension.

He looked at her steadily. Then he said:

"I haven't had an erection for a long time," and in a neutral voice added, "I don't mind. I'm not going to talk about it now or anytime."

Something in his face made her forget about laughing, complaining, protesting, or even taking it too seriously.

"If you want to know," Ecks went on, "I find that there is a kind of harmony in impotence."

She didn't want to know; the words were obscure. Yet she understood them. In fact, she found herself in agreement.

"I shall take my clothes off all the same," Ecks concluded, "because there is no reason why I shouldn't, and because it's very hot in this room."

He undressed, taking care not to wrinkle his clothes; he didn't have many and he needed to take good care of them. He stood naked, the flaccid member between his legs deserving no attention from anyone.

Lying by her side he lit another cigarette and asked her whether she liked dogs.

He left her room with the feeling that something had cleared in his mind. Without knowing why, he felt he was nearer the solution of his dream—that dream which recurred two or three times a week, with the oppressive presence of its enigma for which he had not yet found a precise answer, though he had three or four working hypotheses. Old kings—he repeated—in love with their daughters, propose. Impossible riddles. To naive suitors. Beheaded.

The feeling of relative clarity drove him to walk along the streets of the city in no specific direction; like walking in a museum, unable to find the exact relic, but with the conviction that the timeless smell of dust must lead somewhere. That's how they travelled in the old days: by inaccurate maps with mysterious seas and fantastic monsters, unknown shores and imaginary islands. But in the end the admiral's letter to the king revealed that, in the remote land to which the winds had blown his fleet, gigantic trees grew, as did medicinal herbs and men of another race. Operating on comparisons and imagination.

Brown pigeons stepped in front of him.

The sign on the door said:
SENSATIONAL SPECTACLE
THREE CONTINUOUS SHOWS

OF PORNO-SEX
FABULOUS TRANSVESTITES
ARE THEY MEN OR WOMEN?
SEE THEM AND DECIDE
FOR YOURSELVES
(Adults only)

Ecks looked absentmindedly at the photographs, black and white, background figures flattened by the effect of the flash. But the shiny paper and the street lights gave them a mysterious splendour. Feathers fluttered on the heads of men and women alike, nylon stockings with rhomboid patterns blazed on their legs. Bright-coloured glass sparkled on their necklines, rings rested like butterflies on their fingers.

A sordid stairway led to the hall. Something drew Ecks to look again at the photos. Suddenly he recognized a face and quickly bought a ticket. His eyes clouded over and his hands began to tremble; he did not mind being out of cigarettes. By the door a poorly-dressed man with a raucous voice and equivocal appearance advertised his wares for sale: pornographic postcards, condoms, perfume, lubricating ointments, erotic statuettes, calendars of sporting events, pens with naked girls pictured on the cases. Ecks almost knocked him down as he went by. What is. The greatest tribute. And homage. That a man. Can give. To the woman. He loves.

The show had already started and the lights in the pit were out. Ecks was pleased that there were no ushers because this permitted him to remain standing behind a column. The theatre was small, box-like and without ventilation. It must have been very difficult to see anything from the back rows. The air was unbreathable, the space crowded with men in shirt-sleeves, sweaty and smelling of stale oil. The first row of seats was very close to the stage, to economize on space and also create a kind of intimacy between audience and performers, so that each group would rouse the excitement of the other. The spectators stretched in their seats displayed that false security which comes from numbers and anonymity, the confidence of being paying customers, audience and not performers, breathing noisily, having large bellies, jokes at the ready, and dependable muscular reflexes between their legs. They seemed to have reverted to a stage of infantile impunity in which they felt all-powerful, uninhibited and irresponsible.

They were unknown to each other, yet being all members of the same sex (no women were present) their unity goaded them into being provocative and obscene, indulging in false hilarity. They jeered and taunted, burst inflated paper bags, belched, whistled, applauded, stamped their feet.

The first part was nearly over. Ecks caught sight of Lucía in a group; she wore a top hat over her short blond hair, and wore a tie and baggy flowing trousers; she looked like Charlotte Rampling in *The Night Porter*, imitating Helmut Berger in *Twilight of the Gods*, who was imitating Marlene Dietrich in *The Blue Angel*. She was in fact Marlene Dietrich, the beginning and the end of all imitations; Marlene singing Lili Marlene.

bei der Kaserne
vor dem grossen Tor
steht ein Lanterne
und steht sie noch davor
da wollen wir uns
 wiedersehen

Marlene in tails, top hat and with a long dark cigarette-holder arrives one night in Beverly Hills on the arm of Dolores del Rio. They have come

bui dur Lanterne
wollen wir stehen
wie einst Lili Marlene
wie einst Lili Marlene
und sollte mir ein Lied
  geschehen
wer wird bei der Lanterne
  stehen
mit dir Lili Marlene
mit dir Lili Marlene

for a wedding. Marlene with her boy's breasts under the starched shirt and Dolores del Rio with her loose long hair over her shoulders and a red rose in her décolletage. Marlene with her low voice caressing the words with which she mocks the groom.

Marlene and Dolores drinking champagne (petals in the cups). Marlene in her masculine attire seducing men and women alike. Dolores laughing with a display of splendid white teeth.

Lucía acted Marlene and the other (a man dressed up as a woman, or a woman disguised, someone who had changed identity to assume the identity of a fantasy, someone who had decided to be what s/he wanted to be, and not what s/he was programmed to be) played the role of Dolores del Rio, the Dolores of years ago, with her bold Mexican looks, her full body of a woman accustomed to bulls and fights, and not to the smiles of a summer night. Dolores who awoke the desires of passionate men in a ring of blood and sand, in which Hemingway would have liked to write, Henry Miller to ejaculate (or viceversa). The two women (or the woman and the man) appeared on stage amidst the whistles of the public which demanded that Marlene rape Dolores or that Dolores take Marlene while the strains of Lola-Lola were heard over an old gramophone. "Nobody here may remember Joseph von Sternberg," (Lucía spoke unexpectedly into the microphone), "who took Marlene to the United States where she became the great star, saving her from the Nazi gas chambers"; and then, with deliberate and measured movements she took off her evening jacket and threw it away in the direction of Dolores who was standing at the back of the stage.

The public stopped shouting and whistling: there was a kind of solemn authority—like that of a snake charmer—in the gesture of Lucía's arms encased in the starched shirt, which for a moment succeeded in silencing the rowdy crowd. ("Even brutes are susceptible to the ceremony of her hands," thought Ecks.)

Now she was slowly removing the collar—her soft white fingers collaborating in the delicate operation—and was showing it to the public; cat-calls and hand clapping anticipated the next stage of her act: she began to undo the pearl-like buttons of her shirt, liberating them one by one from the encircling hole; many hands offered help, but Dolores bravely defended the territory: she was not going to allow that, the price of the ticket is for looking, not touching, what did you think, sweetheart? Son or daughter-of-a-bitch, a fan shouted, go on, on!

And Lucía moved on to the cufflinks, decorated with a fleur de lys. She took them off delicately and Dolores picked them up; they were meant for her, but she threw them to the audience, touched (blessed) now by two pairs of hands, hers and Marlene's.

The ceremony continued; now Marlene was beginning to undo the front of her trousers with both hands, releasing the waist-band, slowly at first and then suddenly snapping it open; next each of the fly buttons—invisible yet undoubtedly there—and Dolores' mouth was wet, Dolores brought out her tongue and passed it over her large lips violently painted red, a moan rose from the audience, some pretended to faint, while with her trousers now undone Marlene took one long puff from her black cigarette holder, and another and another, holding the smoke in her throat, then letting it out in concentric oval shapes which floated round, above and dispersed in the hall. Marlene gave back the holder to Dolores who standing in front of her caught the last circle of smoke just as it came out of her mouth, and their lips touched.

The audience shouted for more. Turning her back to them, her trousers hanging lose from the open belt, slipping away from her waist, the shirt tails out, the cuffs open, Marlene began to caress her shoulders—her blond hair did not entirely cover the curve of her head—and the back of her neck. The gramophone went on playing Lola-Lola, red and white lights flickered rapidly across the stage; Marlene was slowly undulating her hips, those small blond hips, and the trousers began to slide down. With a violent movement she ripped off her shirt and cast it away. Still with her back turned, Marlene increased the swinging rythmn of her body in time with the increased speed of the multicoloured lights. The trousers fell down, Marlene stepped outside them, picked them up and threw them at the back of the stage, turned around and appeared completely naked, her round small breasts, her pale nipples, the outline of the blond pubis illuminated, caressed by the white light that slid across her body, her neck, her waist, her legs.

Once again people were silent; Lucía was slowly twisting her limbs—red light on her thighs—moving her arms—white light on her sex—opening her legs—blue light on her face—now she appeared fixed to the ground like a pair of open scissors; and Dolores stealthily approached, her mouth glowing with saliva. Lowered lights heralded her intrusion: hot-blooded Mexican, could anybody have thought that Marlene would mount you?

Dolores advances, a wet obscene animal; white lights swamp Marlene's legs as the dusky arms of Dolores cover them; the tongue flicks out of the mouth, a nervous swift viper: the tongue—painted red so as to be seen from afar—begins to lick slowly and thoroughly, rasping the skin of the legs, moistening the knees, dipping into the thighs, drawing back to impart wetness to areas of the skin insufficiently irrigated. Marlene turns her head from one side to another; now the tongue reaches the outline of the pubis, and the smacking sound of Dolores' avid lips hollows out the hall, echoed by the inhaled breath of her watching public. The blue light nets the blond fuzz, that golden forest; stinging sweet, the spidery tongue pecks and withdraws, advances and retreats. Now it erects itself, displaying a few clinging golden hairs, like a lion exhibiting the remains of the devoured prey; then it returns with sharper purpose to the labia, dipping, twisting and turning, and the light shines on the circle where the tongue enters and delves; the public moan, then roar, a damp patch spreads on the stage. Marlene turns around, lies on her back; Dolores introduces a hand between her legs.

Ecks looked for Lucía's dressing room. When he found it he pushed the door and went in. He now wanted a cigarette. The room was narrow, badly lit by a single yellow candle shining against the torn wallpaper patterned with flowers; a long mirror stained by fly droppings resting upon a wooden chest; various items hanging from a clothes rack, a glass ash-tray full of burnt ends; paper decorations and garlands piled up on a twisted arm-chair with one missing leg; a glass flower vase. There were three or four women; Ecks recognized Lucía: her face was slightly made up, blue lines shadowed her eyes, a false blond moustache created a fine down over her upper lip; she was wearing a pair of close-fitting trousers, a top hat and white gloves; a cigarette burnt on the edge of the full ash-tray.

Lucía turned towards him in surprise. She managed to hide her amazement but a flash of light accentuated the blue of her made-up eyes.

She looked at him intensely for a minute.

Then she said firmly: "Never again."

Ecks remained standing near the door with the pain-ful sensation that the other women were looking at him without curiosity or surprise, as if he were an object, a table or a wardrobe which blocked the entrance.

He then moved towards Lucía (who still wore that fixed look and was murmuring almost imperceptibly, "Never again") and delicately touched her short blond hair which did not reach her ear lobes.

Dressed in men's clothes, the brilliance of her blue eyes accentuated by the dark surrounding line, a little powder on her cheeks and two small earrings, Lucía presented the perfect androgynous image. She looked at Ecks and he felt overpowered by that ambiguity. He saw the unfolding of two parallel worlds in all their splen-dour; two different calls, two messages, two appearances, two perceptions, two languages, yet inseparably con-nected in such a way that the triumph of one would cause the death of both. He was aware that the beauty of one increased the beauty of the other, that two pair of eyes looked at him, four lips whispered, two wonderful heads shone in their harmony. The revelation was unbearable; it suffused everything around him. Yet he needed to be humble in its presence.

"Do you know," his voice had become tender after this inebriating vision, "I am haunted by an enigma in my dreams. There's a recurring, overpowering dream in which an old king in love with his daughter poses a riddle for her suitors (and you appear in my dream as the daughter desired by the father who not daring to call her by her name calls her by that of his queen or one of his concubines). I must solve the riddle, if I am to be worthy of the king's daughter. The riddle goes: What is the greatest tribute and homage a man can give to the woman he loves?

"It is a difficult question; in the dream I am confused, bewildered, slow; I hesitate. I have only one chance to give my answer, and I can't find it. I have thought of possible solutions, perhaps the enigma is based on some trick, it is a trap and the answer could be: 'Do nothing'. But now I know I was wrong; now I have found the answer. Looking at you just now brought it to me; you are the evidence I searched for. When tonight I dream, I shall be able to give my answer. Strangely enough, it has been within me for some time, but I haven't dared pronounce it. Obviously I must say it first to the princess, since she has inspired the enigma. If I give you the right answer, I shall be rid of this tyranny and can speak up in my dream. The answer is, virility."

Old kings in love with their daughters. They invent impossible riddles. Loving suitors. Cannot find the answer. Lose their heads. Old kings. In love with their daughters In the delirium of love. Confuse the name of the queen or of the slave. "What is the greatest tribute and homage a man can give to the woman he loves?" the king asked sternly.

In the dream it is night and Ecks is in an open field; there are no stars, no moon, no trees, no water, no birds, no fish. Only the royal tent in the faraway camp. In the dream, Ecks looks for the king's desired daughter among the shadows in the mist. To be worthy of her means to know the answer. The old father walks proudly in his camp, looks defiantly at the young man, confident that he will never find the solution. But Ecks rises in the dream, his eyes shining with exultation, stealthily approaches the king and word-by-word shouts the answer in his face: "The greatest tribute and homage a man can give to the woman he loves is virility".

Thunder is heard, winged lightning crosses the sky, rocks fall, the earth opens, strange beasts seek refuge in the hills. "Virility!", repeats Ecks; and the king shrinks, is now no bigger than a toy, a paper-maché puppet, a chocolate king; and he falls to the ground, blends with the mud; overcome, beaten, the poor little king disappears. He dies with a whimper.

The tapestry is missing January, November, December
and at least
two of the rivers of Paradise.

About the translator:
PSICHE HUGHES is a London-based specialist in and teacher of Latin American literature. She benefits from a long friendship with the author and a detailed knowledge of her works.

Latin American Titles from Readers International

Sergio Ramírez

TO BURY OUR FATHERS £5.95/US$8.95 paperback

A panoramic novel of Nicaragua in the Somoza era, dramatically recreated by the country's leading prose artist—now also its Vice President. Cabaret singers, exiles, National Guardsmen, guerrillas, itinerant traders, beauty queens, prostitutes and would-be presidents are the characters who people this sophisticated, lyrical and timeless epic of resistance and retribution.

"Very funny, very human, a must for any student of Latin America." *Punch*

"Read slowly and carefully in order to appreciate and absorb all its nuances ...Dr Ramírez is as important as the substantial literary merits of his book." *New York Times Book Review*

"The only contemporary Nicaraguan novel available in English." *Library Journal*

STORIES £3.95/US$7.95 paperback

In these sardonic and moving tales, Sergio Ramírez explores the comic yet painful condition of Latin America, locked into the pursuit of a cruelly elusive and banal "yanqui" culture. In "Charles Atlas Also Dies" a young Nicaraguan becomes a devoted follower of the American bodybuilder, only to discover that age and infirmity have consumed his cult hero. In "To Jackie with All Our Heart" the pretensions of Managua's tiny country club set lead them into a monstrous hoax. In "Saint Nikolaus" a failed Venezuelan student, scratching a living in Berlin, hires himself out as Santa Claus to a rich West German family—only to find himself the target of tensions and jealousies beyond his control.

"Biting and satirical." *The New York Times*

"Masterfully told ... should reach readers' hearts."

Publishers Weekly

"The freshness, force and sheer bite of *Stories* is a complete delight." *Punch*

"Exquisite ... hilarious." *The Guardian*

Antonio Skármeta

I DREAMT THE SNOW WAS BURNING
£4.95/US$7.95 paperback £8.95/US$14.95 hardback

The lodgers at a seedy Santiago boarding house mirror all the warmth and doomed enthusiasm of the last days of Allende, before the fall of democratic Chile brought tanks into the streets, enthroned the generals and turned the national football stadium into a torture centre. The growing political tension fuses with the dreams and evasions of a fleabitten entertainer, the drive of a cynical young country boy to win at football and lose his virginity, and the humbler lives and loves of the other boarders.

"Compelling and entertaining...the most ambitious and accomplished piece of literature to come out of Chile since Pinochet took power." Ariel Dorfman, *Village Voice*

"Imaginative, energetic, and possessed of its own odd charm."
New York Times

"It's easy to see why Latin American and European critics regard this as a Latin American classic of 'committed literature'." *San Francisco Chronicle*

Antônio Torres

THE LAND
£3.95/US$7.95 paperback £8.95/US$14.95 hardback

In this modern Brazilian classic, Torres brings alive the primitive, lyrical world of Brazil's rural *Sertão* (the Backlands of the Northeast). The death of Nelo, a favourite son whom everyone believed had made good in São Paulo, is reflected in the thoughts, dreams and fantasies of his family and neighbours—an interior voyage that takes us to the heart of Brazil's conflict between rural and urban values.

"A sad, simple, lyrical novel...uplifted by Torres' melodic prose and intimate knowledge of rural Brazil." *Kirkus Reviews*

"Full of the unanswered questions of a third-world country in transition." *Publishers Weekly*

"I very much admire the warmth, the irony, the style of *The Land* which so brilliantly describes the lives of poor people in a village whose life is leaving it." Doris Lessing

Latin American Titles from Readers International

Marta Traba

MOTHERS AND SHADOWS
£3.95/US$7.95 paperback   £8.95/US$14.95 hardback

An encounter between two women evokes a decade of tragedy and terror in Latin America's Southern Cone. Irene, a middle-aged actress accustomed to the role of seductress, fears for her son in Chile's newly installed military repression. Dolores has lost her lover and their unborn child to the torturers. Thrown together in a dispirited and cowering Montevideo, the women lead us on, with an unerring sense of place. Out of the horror comes warmth, attachment and the strength to refuse all lies. Now a BBC radio play.

"A well-paced and tense story, building up to the final climactic moment. The translation is superb." *Choice*

"Impressive and very readable, exciting, and Jo Labanyi's fluent translation makes it all imaginable." *Financial Times*

Osvaldo Soriano

A FUNNY DIRTY LITTLE WAR
£3.95/US$6.95 paperback   £7.95/US$12.50 hardback

"*A Funny Dirty Little War* is an absolute of its kind: the attempt of one petty official to oust another farcically, inexorably, horribly sweeps a small Argentine town into a local holocaust of violence and murder...it is as if the amiable village world of Don Camillo were blackened by the laconic ugliness of Hemingway's war writing." John Updike, *The New Yorker*

"The black humour, dizzying action, crisp, sparkling dialogue, the rapid unemotional style...make this novel gripping reading."
Italo Calvino

"A gripping fable of power and revolution...its message is universal." *ALA Booklist*

"Masterful juxtaposition of farce and tragedy...a worthy addition to collections of modern Latin American fiction."
Library Journal

READ THE WORLD—Books from Readers International

Nicaragua	**To Bury Our Fathers**	Sergio Ramírez	£5.95/US$8.95
Nicaragua	**Stories**	Sergio Ramírez	£3.95/US$7.95
Chile	**I Dreamt the Snow Was Burning**	Antonio Skármeta	£4.95/US$7.95
Brazil	**The Land**	Antônio Torres	£3.95/US$7.95
Argentina	**Mothers and Shadows**	Marta Traba	£3.95/US$7.95
Argentina	**A Funny Dirty Little War**	Osvaldo Soriano	£3.95/US$6.95
Uruguay	**El Infierno**	C. Martínez Moreno	£4.95/US$8.95
Haiti	**Cathedral of the August Heat**	Pierre Clitandre	£4.95/US$8.95
Congo	**The Laughing Cry**	Henri Lopes	£4.95/US$8.95
Angola	**The World of 'Mestre' Tamoda**	Uanhenga Xitu	£4.95/US$8.95
S. Africa	**Fools and Other Stories**	Njabulo Ndebele	USA only $8.95
S. Africa	**Renewal Time**	Es'kia Mphahlele	£4.95/US$8.95
S. Africa	**Hajji Musa and the Hindu Fire-Walker**	Ahmed Essop	£4.95/US$8.95
Iran	**The Ayatollah and I**	Hadi Khorsandi	£3.95/US$7.95
Philippines	**Awaiting Trespass**	Linda Ty-Casper	£3.95/US$7.95
Philippines	**Wings of Stone**	Linda Ty-Casper	£4.95/US$8.95
Japan	**Fire from the Ashes**	ed. Kenzaburō Ōe	£3.50 UK only
China	**The Gourmet**	Lu Wenfu	£4.95/US$8.95
India	**The World Elsewhere**	Nirmal Verma	hbk only £9.95/US$16.95
Poland	**Poland Under Black Light**	Janusz Anderman	£3.95/US$6.95
Poland	**The Edge of the World**	Janusz Anderman	£3.95/US$7.95
Czech.	**My Merry Mornings**	Ivan Klíma	£4.95/US$7.95
Czech.	**A Cup of Coffee with My Interrogator**	Ludvík Vaculík	£3.95/US$7.95
E. Germany	**Flight of Ashes**	Monika Maron	£4.95/US$8.95
E. Germany	**The Defector**	Monika Maron	£4.95/US$8.95
USSR	**The Queue**	Vladimir Sorokin	£4.95/US$8.95

Order through your local bookshop, or direct from the publisher. Most titles also available in hardcover. *How to order:* Send your name, address, order and payment to

RI, 8 Strathray Gardens, London NW3 4NY, UK

or **RI**, P.O. Box 959, Columbia, LA 71418, USA

Please enclose payment to the value of the cover price plus 10% of the total amount for postage and packing. (Canadians add 20% to US prices.)